OUTLANDER

STORIES AND ESSAYS

BY
JANE RULE

OUTLANDER
by
JANE RULE

the Naiad Press inc.
1982

ACKNOWLEDGMENTS

"Home Movie" first appeared in *Sinister Wisdom*; "The Day I Don't Remember" in *Rara Avis*; "The Outlander" in *Canadian Fiction Magazine*; "Miss Wistan's Promise," "In the Attic of the House," and "First Love/Last Love" in *Christopher Street*; "Pictures" under another title in *The Ladder*, revised in the *Body Politic*; "Lilian" in *Conditions II*, "Sightseers in Death Valley" on *Anthology*, Canadian Broadcasting Corporation.

"Sexuality in Literature" first appeared in *Fireweed*, "With All Due Respect" in *After You're Out*, "Homophobia and Romantic Love" in *Conditions III*, "Grandmothers" in *Lavender Culture*; all other essays first appeared in the *Body Politic*.

Printed in the United States of America
First Edition
First Printing, April, 1981
Second Printing, June, 1981
Third Printing, August, 1982

Cover design by Tee A. Corinne

ISBN: 0-930044-17-7

Library of Congress Catalog Card Number: 80-84221

Design and typesetting in Janson by Annie Graham Co., Iowa City.

For Avis Seads

Other Works by Jane Rule

1964 Desert of the Heart
1970 This Is Not for You
1971 Against the Season
1975 Lesbian Images
1975 Theme for Diverse Instruments
1977 The Young in One Another's Arms
1980 Contract with the World

About the Author

JANE RULE WAS born in Plainfield, New Jersey in 1931, grew up in the midwest and in California, and graduated from Mills College, California, in 1952. In 1956, she moved to Vancouver, British Columbia, where she and Helen Sonthoff lived, teaching and writing, for twenty years, spending summers in England, Greece, or New England. They have spent the last five years on Galiano Island, off the coast of British Columbia, taking a winter month or two on the southern deserts of California or Arizona. A Canadian citizen for some years, Jane Rule is active in the writers', women's and gay communities, reviewing books, writing articles, and serving on government committees; but writing fiction continues to be her chief occupation.

photo by Tee A. Corinne

Contents

Stories

Home Movie

ALYSOUN CARR SAT at a table in a street cafe in Athens drinking ouzo. Directly across from her, through an open window and onto a far wall, a home movie was being projected. A young couple grew larger on the wall. Suddenly the enormous head of a baby filled the whole window, as if it were going to be born into the street. Alysoun, careful in a foreign country never to make so melodramatic a gesture as to cover her eyes if she could help it, looked away. She added water to the ouzo and watched what had been clear thick liquid thin and turn milky. She did not like the licorice aftertaste, but she liked the effect, which was a gentling of her senses so that she could receive things otherwise too bright or loud or pungent at a level of tolerance, even pleasure. In another ten minutes, if the movie lasted so long, she could watch it without dismay.

At her own home, such a show could go on as long as an hour if absolutely everything her father had ever taken was resurrected for the occasion and supplemented by an ancient cartoon or two he'd bought for a forgotten birthday of one of the children. At least two of the films were always also shown backwards, causing a hysteria of giggles in which, at least for Alysoun, there was an element of alarm. It was daunting to see how without effort the projector could do what all the king's horses and all the king's men could not, the diver's feet breaking the water and restoring him by impossible magnetism to the board, the child toppling up onto the chair "to keep the past upon its throne," where did that come from? Another wall. The camera, particularly the movie camera, is reactionary. It doesn't have to run backwards to prove its point. Alysoun always dreaded most the moment when her own baby face would fill the frame, and her father would say, "Well, you're all good-looking kids, but Alysoun was the prettiest baby I ever saw." Alysoun could never see why, a head with that little hair, offering up not a smile but a silent snort as if blowing a nose without a handkerchief directly into the camera. The remark could have made the others jealous if the past tense wasn't emphasized as a rebuke. Her father seemed to see the process of her growing up as some horribly disfiguring disease or mortal accident. Only the camera could give him back that pretty baby who, snorting out at her adult self, made Alysoun feel as disoriented as if she had been physically dragged by the camera back up out of the water and onto the springing board. Others of her siblings had reproduced; Alysoun had not. Perhaps her father was only complaining that she hadn't given him the pleasure a second time in life, a granddaughter about whom he could say, "She's almost as pretty as her mother." Only by having children were you allowed by such a parent to go on living in the present.

Alysoun looked back through the window at remarkably bad views of what might have been a flower garden. A film maker has no business trembling with awe before anything, but what ten minutes ago would have made Alysoun mildly nauseated now amused her. People talked about the universality of great art, but far more universal is the mark of an amateur, trapping all he loves in the cage of his own unpracticed seeing and letting it run backwards out of time. If she had watched long enough, surely a Greek diver's feet would break the water, a Greek baby snort; but Alysoun could not wait. She was due at a rehearsal, and she had to stop at the hotel to pick up her instrument.

The walk back down the steep street, loud with Greek and aggressive automobiles, would dissipate the mild sedative her drink had been and leave her ready to do what she always did very well, whether alone or before an audience.

"Don't you ever have stage fright?" her father demanded before her first important appearance with the San Francisco Symphony. For Alysoun to be able to go into the high calm she could always achieve when she was about to confront any music was, if not inhuman, shockingly insensitive for a woman.

She did not tell him that she was frightened of nearly everything else: what most people were afraid of, like getting on an airplane or meeting vicious dogs; what some people were afraid of, like sex or fortune-tellers; what no one should be afraid of, like eating or her

father. She did not tell him because at the moment before a perform-
ance she did not have to be afraid of anything

Everyone with whom she must play had practiced, as she had, for
years, read from the same score, followed the same conductor. Together they were in agreement, in control of what happened. Having
discovered that cooperative security very young, Alysoun never
wanted to leave it for the reality outside music, at which she'd never
known how to practice, for which there seemed to be neither agreed
score nor conductor. Each time she played, she was inside that universal harmony toward which life and even the other arts struggled
but only music achieved.

Only after the rehearsal, on her way to a midnight dinner, listening
to flamboyant concertmaster say, "Such control! Such feeling! You
play to my soul!" Alysoun wondered if she would vomit or faint in
the street or burst into hysterical tears. More often, like tonight,
she managed to control herself enough to make it to the restaurant,
only to stare at a dinner no hunger could have forced her to eat,
while the concertmaster protested at American vanity that made their
women thin as even the poor would be ashamed to be in Greece.

"You are no bigger around than your own clarinet!"

The criticism was modestly reassuring; it meant her dinner partner
was more offended by her skeletal thinness than attracted by the
novelty of her blond hair, and she could soon go to her bed without argument.

"But she is famous even in her own country as the lady who does
not eat," said a young woman sitting across from Alysoun, who had
been introduced as the sister to the first viola.

"How do you know that?" Alysoun demanded.

"I read about you at the American Information Center. I work for
the Americans as a translator."

There had been a hushed-up episode when, after one of her col-
lapses, an ordinary doctor rather than a psychiatrist had been called.
Instead of being diagnosed as an unfocused phobic for whom little
could be done, or being told she suffered the absolutely normal anxieties of a career woman who should marry, stay home, and have a
baby, she was informed that she was suffering from malnutrition.
She went into the hospital to be fed intravenously until she could

tolerate the sight of food. In the protected environment of the hospital, Alysoun had done very•well. She put on ten pounds and left with the knowledge that, though she had not found a cure, she had found a retreat. Then her doctor, pleased, no doubt, with the shadow of breasts that could now be discerned under her blouse, feeling in a creative way responsible for them, asked her to marry him.

Alysoun had learned not to say in response that she didn't like sex; it was too much of a challenge. None of her other real reasons was much help either, for men could easily delude themselves that, servile in pursuit, they could be servile masters. She had to invent her excuse.

"I not only read you do not eat but that you have a mysterious lover. Some say a great head of state, some say a reclusive millionaire," sister to the viola went on, and her eyes, though not unfriendly, were disbelieving.

"I must try to get some sleep," Alysoun said. "I haven't got over the time change."

Their immediate, effusive sympathy might have been a taunting protest, the way her throat soured. She was trembling.

"I will take you," the young woman offered. "I have a car right there."

"Thank you. I didn't even catch your name."

"Constantina. It must be dreadful for you, having to do this after every rehearsal, all over the world. Oh, they play like angels, I am the first to admit, but they eat like beasts and talk like men. Tomorrow night I'm going to kidnap you and take you somewhere quiet where you can have fresh fish and salad, and I will not talk to you or even look at you if you prefer. I hope you have forgiven me for gossiping about you to you, but it did stop them, yes?"

Because Constantina was concentrating on moments of inexcusable traffic, Alysoun could watch her throughout her monologue, a high, very white forehead against her dark hair and straight dark brows, a rather sharp nose, a very wide mouth with handsome white teeth. No one would call her pretty; no one would easily forget her face. She was about thirty, Alysoun's own age.

"And lunch. May I take you to lunch? Before you decide, I warn you that it is because I want to make use of you, and I can tell by looking at you that you know what I need to know."

"I know about nearly nothing but music," Alysoun said.

"You know the names of flowers," Constantina said.

"Yes," Alysoun admitted.

"Then you must have lunch with me, as an official duty, a matter of good will between nations."

"Thank you. I'd like that."

In a strange bed, where she could be afraid of sleep in certain states of exhaustion, Alysoun wondered why such overt flattery had pleased rather than offended her, why she had responded so confidently about her knowledge of flowers when it was her habit always to deny anything that she could, to avoid being known, to avoid obligation. Enduring the endless novelty of anxieties was, if not easier, at least less humiliating alone. She could always resort to practicing, even just the fingering if other people might be disturbed. Something in Constantina's confidence was specifically protective of Alysoun without a trace of inevitable male condescension; and Constantina had had the good sense to ask a favor, one it would give Alysoun pleasure to grant, for she had learned the names of flowers very early in her vocabulary, where they stayed certain and bright, a gift from her mother, who could forget the name of a child or neighbor but never the precise definition of a tulip or rhododendron or rose. In memory no film had ever picked from her, Alysoun, not much more than flower-high, walked with her mother naming the last of the Daffodils—Carlton, King Alfred—and the early tulips—White Triumphator, General de Wet. Naming was better than counting, which could start tomorrow night's concert in her head. She was walking, nearly hidden in rhododendrons, saying, "Unique, Pink Pearl, Sappho . . ." when she slept. It was noon when she woke.

Constantina was waiting for her in the lobby, rose and came to her quickly, embraced her formally and stood back "You have slept."

"Yes, thank you, very well," Alysoun said, "thinking of my mother's flower garden."

"Very good. I have a plan. We can walk, shall we? It is all right for you? It is not far, to the old Placa. We will have lunch, very simple, nothing much. Then we will do our work. We will go to the flower vendors. I will tell you the name of the flower; you will pick it out, and then the vendor will tell me its name in Greek."

"What is this for?" Alysoun asked.

"Oh, I am translating a collection of Eudora Welty's short stories for the American Information Center. They are *full* of flowers."

Alysoun was grateful to have heard of Eudora Welty, remembered that she had read a story or two of hers but could not remember what.

"I am embarrassed not to know the flowers in Greek. When Yaya taught us, I had my head in a book," Constantina confessed without guilt. "And they are not listed so particularly as I need in Greek-English dictionaries."

Alysoun had to concentrate to hear what Constantina was saying because they were also negotiating the noon crowds along the narrow sidewalks, up onto which cars swerved without concern for pedestrians. Constantina had a cautious aggression Alysoun felt she could trust; so she followed, let her arm be taken, even allowed herself to be pushed ahead of Constantina until they escaped through a dark doorway and down a narrow hall. There had not been a sign Alysoun could see.

"How does anyone know this is a restaurant?"

"I don't know. It's just always been here, and we have always come to it," Constantina said, directing her into a room of perhaps eighteen tables, two or three already taken by groups of men. "I am sorry we may be the only women here, but we will be left alone, and the food is safe for Americans. Shall I order for you?"

As in the car the night before, Alysoun had an opportunity to study Constantina's face while she read the menu, behaving as if it were in a foreign language she must translate for herself. She had the kind of face that registered every small perplexity and pleasure but might be a busy mask for deeper moods and needs. When she had made a choice, she described it in detail to Alysoun, who agreed at once.

"You know, it's not that I don't like to eat. It's just sometimes I can't."

"I understand. I understand exactly," Constantina said. "One can feel such a victim to food."

"Do you often have to take visiting Americans around?" Alysoun asked, for she knew how notoriously small Greek salaries were against their social obligations; the only country that was worse was Japan.

"Unfortunately, no. I am no one of importance, after all. I met you because my brother is kind to me, and he understood my urgency. He even allowed me to use his car. I do not want to sound like a schoolgirl. I have your record. I admire it very much, and you. That is enough of my confession. Are you who you are because you obeyed your parents' wishes?"

"No," Alysoun said. "Oh, they've come round by now, of course. And they might have come round sooner if I'd played the violin or the viola or the piano or even the flute."

"Or the harp?"

Alysoun laughed and said, "That might have seemed to them a little excessive. And the clarinet isn't as bad as the cello or French horn would have been."

"I can hardly bear to watch a woman playing the cello myself. But what could be the objection to the clarinet?"

"It probably didn't have to do with the instrument. I wanted to learn to play it because my best friend did. My father never liked influences on his children other than his own . . . or Mother's, of course."

"What was your friend's name?"

"Bobby Anne. I haven't thought of Bobby Anne in years!"

"How faithless you are, when she inspired your whole career!"

"But I discovered in the process that it was the clarinet rather than Bobby Anne I loved."

"The true obsession is always work," Constantina said.

"Do you know that?" Alysoun asked, surprised. "It isn't really like a discipline at all. It's much more like a habit, impossible to give up. Not that I want to give it up, but I don't think I could. My father said it was giving me buckteeth just as if I were sucking my thumb. My brother started calling me Bugs Bunny. Even Mother thought I should have braces."

"And you did?"

"No, as you can see. My music teacher said minor vanities had to be sacrificed, and I didn't really care as long as I could go on playing, and that was before I even learned to like music."

"You have beautiful teeth," Constantina insisted. "How different it

is for my brother. He is doing what my parents want. He never
learned to like music. It is nothing but work, work, work; and he is
bored—bored to his soul."

"How terrible!"

"Yet he is loved, oh so loved! And they go on helping him."

"Don't they help you?" Alysoun asked. "Don't they approve of
what you're doing?"

"No. Oh, they don't mind so much now, but my father used to call
English the devil's tongue, probably because my mother speaks it
well. I simply outlasted him. My greatest strength is my attention
span. He finally just lost interest in his own objections and let me
come to Athens . . . to keep house for my brother, of course."

"Will you marry?"

"Never!" Constantina said. "My brother, he wants to marry, but I
tell him incest is all he will ever be able to afford."

"Do you have to live with him?"

"I don't mind," Constantina said. "He is a kind man, but one day
when he does marry, I look forward to living alone . . . or with a
friend."

"A friend?"

"You have no lover," Constantina stated, suddenly changing the
subject.

"I like the way you make statements rather than ask questions. I
let people think I do. It's the only refusal that seems to make sense
to anyone."

"You have enjoyed your lunch."

"Yes, I have, and, Constantina, I'd like to pay for it and for dinner,
too. I have a generous travel allowance for this tour, thanks to the
State Department, and there's no reason for you . . . "

Constantina put a hand out to stop this attempt. "If I told you I
had saved for months, looking forward; if I told you what a
privilege . . . ?"

"If I told you I have such a horror of obligation that I usually refuse all invitations . . . ?"

"If I told you the waiter would judge me for failing in Greek hospitality . . . ?"

"If I told you . . . " Alysoun tried to continue, but she was laughing and could think of nothing more to protest.

"Come," Constantina said, "and name me the flowers. Then I will be obliged to you."

The crowds had thinned now, and they had no difficulty strolling arm in arm. Alysoun did not even care that they turned heads and inspired comments. Sometimes Constantina answered back at some length.

"What are you saying?"

"Sometimes I say, 'Go home to your mother and kill a pig,' sometimes much worse."

"Isn't that dangerous?"

"It is nothing. It is like, in a village, saying 'good afternoon.' It is a circumstance where it is rude not to be rude. They are only admiring your hair."

Alysoun, accompanied by a man, felt not so much protected as invisible, and she sometimes wondered if her need to vomit or scream was a fear not of the dangers of the street but of obliteration. With Constantina she had the odd, lighthearted sense of being conspicuous and safe.

When they arrived at the Placa, some of the flower vendors were closing their stands for the afternoon, but there were still at least a dozen open for business, displaying a remarkable variety of flowers.

"Of course, it's May," Alysoun reminded herself. "Greece is like California: absolutely everything blooms in May."

"One story is set in San Francisco. She is describing the San Francisco flower stalls."

"Give me your list."

Looking down it, Alysoun had not seen quite that style of script before and realized Constantina must have learned to write English script once she was old enough to control it and form a conscious style of her own.

"What is the matter? Is it hard to read?"

"No, not at all. I was admiring it. It is very like you," Alysoun said, aware that she was falling into Constantina's habit of compliment.

There were thirty-six flowers on the list. At the first vendor, Alysoun found five of them: carnation, dutch iris, narcissus, begonia, gladiola; and when Constantina explained to the man what they were doing, he gave Constantina not only the Greek name but the flowers, itself and refused payment. With the second vendor, where Alysoun found another four—violet, sweet pea, anemone, amaryllis—it was the same. Soon all the vendors in the Placa knew what the women were doing and called out their specialties in hope of offering the rarer, the lovelier; but only when Alysoun actually saw what she wanted were the Greek names any use to them. The bouquet in Constantina's arms grew larger and more absurdly various, fragrances of rose, iris, lily, a startlingly perfumed orange tulip, more pungent. In a short while they had twenty-five varieties of flowers, sometimes as many as half-a-dozen specimens. The vendors shouted in pleasure.

"Oh, it's getting late," Constantina said, in sudden distress, "and you must rest before the concert."

"I'd forgotten all about the concert," Alysoun confessed, but what would have been truer to say was that she had not needed to think about, consciously keep it in mind as a safe goal to get her through the anxieties of the day.

"A Eudora Welty bouquet," Constantina said, her face disappearing into the blooms. "I am a little in love with her, too."

"By now, so am I," Alysoun said. "I wish we could send it to her or at least let her know. It must be odd to be a writer, never in the presence of the pleasure you give."

At the hotel, they lingered a moment in the lobby.

"I've had such a lovely time," Alysoun said.

"You must have the flowers."

Alysoun began to protest; then instead she simply smiled and took them.

"I'll come for you tonight after the concert," Constantina said, and she was gone.

Alysoun went to her room and rang room service for a vase. The maid looked critically at the flowers and returned with three vases, but the flowers could not be separated. Alysoun chose the largest and began to arrange the bouquet Eudora Welty had called to life. Perhaps when Alysoun was through, she would actually sit down and write Eudora Welty a letter. Constantina would know her publisher. A tulip, deep purple enough to be called black, named Queen of the

Night, was the color of Constantina's eyes; an apricot rose the texture and color of her skin. Now walking along the street, she would be carrying the fragrance that filled this room. Alysoun imagined herself saying to Constantina that night, "If I could have a perfume made of this, I would wear it the rest of my life." And some time after that Constantina would say, "You have loved a woman." And Alysoun would say, "Yes, but such a long time ago she is even less real to me than Bobby Anne." "How faithless you are!" And Alysoun would say . . .

Fear woke in her womb, feeling so like desire that if someone very loving, very skillful had been there at that moment to hold her, to touch her, she would not have resisted. Constantina.

"Dear Eudora Welty," Alysoun began a letter she knew she would neither finish nor mail. "Perhaps it is as well you don't know all the pleasure you give or the insight you bring. I have no idea whether you've ever written a story about this, but because of a bouquet of your flowers (I'll explain what I mean about that in a minute) I've discovered that fear *is* desire, not shame or guilt or inadequacy or any of those other things. The question to ask about fear is not what are you afraid of but what do you want. If you know what you want and you can have it, then fear doesn't seem like fear at all . . . ."

If Alysoun could walk out at the end of the concert tonight not betrayed back into the threatening loneliness of people who only moments before belonged to the same great affirmation of order and harmony and now had nothing to share but petty, conflicting appetites; if instead she were to be with Constantina, who read a menu like a score, who turned an afternoon into a bouquet of flowers, Alysoun might practice to live as she had learned to work, in the high calm of anticipation and presence.

She did not walk out for her solitary drink to watch a world behaving as if everyone were taking part in a home movie, jerky and self-conscious, to be projected over and over again so much larger than life on the flawed wall of childhood. She stayed alone and quiet in her room until it was time to go.

Alysoun Carr played that night as well as she had ever played in her life. Only when she was taking her bow was she aware of the cameras. The concert was being televised not only for the Greek audience but also for Americans who at that moment were watching her image by satellite on their television screens. Her father, her mother, her brothers and sisters would all be together, and for one dangerous second she was tempted to snort before, instead, she smiled her full, bucktoothed, professional smile through a rain of flowers her mother had taught her to name.

The Day I Don't Remember

"YOU INVENT YOUR mother to suit your own guilt!" I shouted. "She's *unreal*."

Jean, her back to me, knelt by the living room bookcase packing up *Rubyfruit Jungle, Lesbian/Woman*, Adrienne Rich's essays. Beside her was a box already full of copies of *Lesbian Tide*, the *Body Politic, Conditions*. And this was only the beginning. It was the third visit in so many years her mother and much younger sister had made to the coast, the third time Jean had packed up all incriminating evidence of our life together. The first time I helped not only with the books and records but with the pictures, and we rearranged our clothes in the closets. I even put our toothbrushes as far from each other as possible in the holder. Orphaned at ten, I was without experience in tending the sensibilities of a mother, and I was, anyway, newly in love and awed by the experience. The second time I got sick, and Jean had to sleep with me whether anyone liked it or not. This time I was being resolutely combative.

"Do you hear me?" I demanded, sounding like somebody's mother myself.

"You like my mother; my mother likes you. Kinky's only fourteen . . . " Jean began, still going on with the witch-hunt through the shelves.

"Fourteen is old enough for the facts of life." If I hadn't known how offended Jean was by details of my boarding school initiation, I would have used my own experience. Instead I tried a trade-off. "I slept alone in a room full of crucifixes when we visited her house, and she's not even Catholic."

"But she had to raise us Catholic."

"She said she didn't mind that you didn't go anymore. She said she'd kept her promise."

"Karin, it would *kill* Mother."

"I don't believe it!" I shouted. "I believe you think it would kill you to admit I matter to you."

"That's not fair," Jean said, giving me her full attention and judgment at the same time.

"Is this?" I asked with a gesture toward the boxes. "We're not even illegal. We're consenting adults."

"For two weeks I also have to be my mother's child."

People deprived early of their mothers are supposed to keep looking for substitutes, but I am frankly embarrassed by any attempt to mother me. That didn't stop me from feeling jealous of Jean, yea, and jealous of her mother, too. Though I was arguing for honesty, loyalty was the real issue. It was time Jean chose me above everyone else, particularly her mother.

"Well, I'm not your mother's child, and I'm not going to lie to her anymore."

I hadn't expected Jean finally to give in. Never having had to come out to a mother myself, I couldn't really imagine how Jean would do it. I just needed to rage around enough for her to know how I felt. Her suggestion that I leave took me totally by surprise. The line went over and over again in my head every day: "Then maybe you'd better find some place to stay . . . ."

What if I'd gone on arguing as if what she had said were no worse than her packing up the books? Or what if I'd admitted I was pushing her too hard and actually right then apologized? I was so taken aback I simply asked, "Do you mean that?" And she said, "Yes."

I didn't pack much. Actually, as I looked around, there wasn't much in the place that belonged to me. Jean's the one to buy things; I'm more apt to spend money on dinners out, weekends away. We'd been here three years, and I was only now noticing that it didn't look like our place at all. It was Jean's, and she was ordering me out of it, just a week before Christmas.

I should have quit my job and left town, gone somewhere I didn't know anybody or taken one of those cruises gay travel agents are always advertising. Only strangers would have patience for my load of anger and self-pity. But I didn't. I slept on one friend's couch until *her* mother arrived. I drank myself out of welcome at another's. On Christmas Eve I put myself up for grabs at the Crossroads and got the

kind of sexual punishment I was probably looking for. I don't remember Christmas day.

I don't even know what day after that it was—Sunday, I guess, because I wasn't at work—I spent hours walking along the beach.
Though Jean's mother was the only argument we've ever had that I
had lost, I knew the ten days behind me were strewn with similar
defeats once Jean had an opportunity to discover and label them. As
one of my erstwhile friends had crudely pointed out, I had been shit-
ting in my own front yard.

"Let her try being holier-than-thou!" I shouted.

"Are you going back then?" the same friend asked.

I didn't know what to answer. I hadn't thought. Trying to, I wasn't
sure I had that option now. Once I was suspended from school and
behaved with so little repentance that I went back to find myself
expelled. Why hadn't *I* told *Jean* to leave? She had a house full of
crucifixes, a mother and a sister to go home to. My ex-guardian
was an uncle who sent me a perpetual subscription to the *New Yorker*
and let the bank deal with the rest. Maybe I should have spent Christmas in the vault.

I should have got Jean Tee Corinne's *Cunt Coloring Book* to open
on Christmas morning, and let her figure out how to be her mother's
child after that! They weren't even my books and records she was
hiding. They were her own. That was the sort of stupid hypocrite
she was, and I was at least going to go back and tell her so.

Jean's mother and Kinky always left the morning of New Year's
Eve. The first year, after we drove them to the airport, we spent the
rest of the day in bed and didn't make it to the party we had planned
to go to. The second year I was already in bed, and Jean spent the
day cleaning and putting everything back in place, the evening playing Olivia records and saying she was sorry. We both were. This
year I turned up around three in the afternoon. I left my suitcase in
the car. I rang the bell.

"Have you lost your key?" she asked when she opened the door.

"No," I said.

I was going to go on to say I didn't feel as if I lived here anymore,
but it all looked so familiar, books and magazines in place, so ordinary
and real, that I asked instead, "When did they leave?"

"The day after they got here," Jean said.

"What?"

"I told them," Jean said.

"Why? Why did you do a crazy thing like that?"

"It's what you wanted me to do."

"But not without me, not without figuring out how so—you know—they wouldn't mind."

"I guess I didn't care by then whether they minded or not," she said, sounding not angry so much as resigned.

"What did she say? What did your mother say?"

"Nothing much. That Kinky was still her responsibility. In Dad's memory, she couldn't accept or condone . . . that sort of thing. Just what you'd expect."

"Why didn't you let me know? Why didn't you call me at work?"

"I don't know," Jean said.

"What did you do for Christmas?"

"Nothing."

"Why?"

"I knew what you were doing."

"I can't remember the day at all," I said, and it couldn't have sounded like an alibi.

"Well," Jean said, "here's all your mail."

I started to open it, not knowing what else to do. Christmas cards seemed horribly beside the point. It could have been March or April. Then I came to the most recent *New Yorker* cover, a reindeer with birds in its antlers.

"Christ!" I said, and I could feel Jean, the ex-Catholic, flinch. "As out-of-key with the season as I am."

She didn't laugh. I felt more inappropriate than ever. "What do you need me to say?"

After a moment, she said, "It's what I need unsaid."

"Why did you do it?"

"Because you were right."

I was surprised into a hope that I might be allowed to be self-righteous all over again, but something about the way Jean held her shoulders warned me not to capitalize on it.

"I could have been more tactful," I said.

"Why did you leave?"

"You said you meant it."

"Maybe I did. But I was very sorry—too sorry. I more or less threw Mother and Kinky out, too."

I was sorry, too, but I hadn't been here to live through it with her. Anything I did or said would make it worse rather than better. What if I said, "You know, I wasn't being honest; I was being jealous"? Jean would just be sorrier than ever.

"Why do you always believe me?" I asked.

"I don't know. I really don't know. Tell your next lover not to believe a word you say."

"You, too," I said. "And tell her . . . "

But I had no advice, even angry. If there had been less room for me when Mom (I did call her "Mom") and Kinky were around, their absence left no room for me at all. Crowding in instead were these two new lovers between whom the reconciliations would have to take place. Jean and I had got past forgiving or skipped it, maybe on that Christmas Day she sat alone refusing to phone, the day I don't remember.

The Puppet Show

I ASSUMED IT was a tragedy, my husband having other women. I told him that it made me feel like a thing. Actually I'd felt like a thing for months, for years before I got hold of that reason for it and could stop feeling guilty and start feeling righteously indignant. I was not to blame. He was. *They were:* sweet declension of the verb *to be*, which right away gave me a small but new measure of self-respect. That's too strong a word for it. The space between a wrong woman and a wronged woman is very small, but I could draw breath, enough to ask for a divorce. He'd been home so little, he hardly knew he had a child, except for the bills he paid at the end of the month; and he was willing to go on being that kind of a father. He knew I could go back to work.

I grew up a planner, not a thinker. Ideas were fine as long as they didn't get in my way, which I wanted to be as clear in the world as it was in my head. I was going to be a nurse so that I could marry a doctor, to have three children, the third both a status symbol and an insurance policy in case an incompetent baby-sitter boiled or drowned or broke one while I was away at a medical convention with my husband. The first year in college, I had a roommate named Bobo, who brooded over courses in philosophy, literature, political science, anthropology, sociology, complaining the while that they were all simply "man's frail systems of defense." Why bother with them then, I wanted to know. What use were they? What did she want out of life? "To understand," Bobo said. I thought that was hilarious. She didn't laugh about my taking golf and tennis and sailing as seriously as I did chemistry, but she wanted to discuss the difference between "outer and inner direction." *"In* means *down* in my book," I said. *"Out* means *up."* Once she asked me, "Are you really at all interested in sick people?" As if I should have a social preference for them in order to be a nurse! Nobody is interested in sick people, least of all their relatives and lovers. Look at all those TV shows, even the news. People are almost as interested in what you go to bed with as who you go to bed with; and what you die of is probably more interesting than who you married. That's not an idea; that's a fact. Bobo was shocked by it. I wasn't. I wanted to be a nurse to marry a doctor to have three kids, and that was enough for me, along with the golf and sailing and tennis.

There were students like Bobo in nursing, too, not so kind and kinky, but humorless and critical, first of the courses, then of the hospital, head nurses and doctors. That type never bitched about the patients, but they didn't last long either, went out with wrenched backs because some three-hundred-pound glutton had as much right to be free of bedsores as the next guy, went out in social protest because some half-dead alcoholic didn't get priority in kidney treatment, went out because they couldn't stand to know how ugly people can be in pain, how hard and pointless dying is. I didn't like some of it myself, but I wasn't surprised about having to put up with being bored or terrified or sick to my stomach or sorry as part of the job.

I *was* shocked to find out that being bored and terrified and sick to my stomach and sorry were part of being married, too. I wonder if Bobo had been around at the time to ask me, "Are you really at all interested in this man?" I'd have thought that was as irrelevant a question as being interested in sick people. He was a doctor. And for him? I was a tough little nurse who knew the realities of life, the endless dirty joke of the body, that flesh puppet of the trade, manipulated for the mastery of it, set aside and forgotten, whether it finally broke down or mended. Being married was like being a chronic patient, needing the same operation performed three or four times a week, a mortal bore for a doctor whose only variety in work is new flesh each time which might occasionally present surprises.

Maybe having a child, a girl child, was the beginning of it, not of being a thing, but of knowing I was, and knowing she would be, the moment she was born into the doctor's hands. We had to call her Elizabeth, for his mother, but I never called her anything but Bobo, because from the moment I first saw her, there out of my hands, she was asking me Bobo's sorts of questions, which didn't then strike me funny at all, and I reached out to take her back to me. I never knew what my own flesh meant until I held her, knowing the person of her body, the will of her arching back and tight fists and imperious cry

The plan for three children had been canceled before Bobo was born. I hadn't even wanted her, a product of the scientific method, a test of my organs. Loving her the way I did didn't change my mind about other children, because I felt so guilty to have forced her into the world to grow up the tough child of a couple of tough people who had no wonder in the world but her. Postpartum depression was my first moral experience; and, though I waited five years for the courage to act on it and even then had to believe I was a victim, she was a question about living I had to answer somehow.

Graduating from marriage isn't like graduating from nursing school, except for having to find a job, night shift this time because I no longer had any illusions about social life, because insomnia is useful in the daytime if you have a five-year-old daughter, because there is not as much manipulating to do during the night, no doctor's visits, no preparation for operations, no bathing and feeding. On a good night, you only have to be watchful and good with a needle. On a bad night, you need to be cheerful-numb.

There is an old woman in a humiliated rage because she's wet her bed. I tell her it's normal; it's the medicine, nothing to worry about. I'll change the bed. But why would any doctor do that to her, she wants to know, shame her like that? It's normal, it's the medicine; it's nothing to be ashamed about. She won't understand me; she won't be quiet. She's waking the other patients. Head nurse says put in a catheter. Two of us, then three of us are trying to reason with her, hold her legs apart, get the catheter into place. She is shouting in a deep, childish voice, "It's *my* body. It's *my* body." I give up, knowing what the sound of pain would be even if I managed. Weeping about a wet bed isn't as noisy.

I take a shot in to a woman who has just had a hysterectomy, am surprised by her face, young, younger than I am, large, dark eyes.

"She's right, you know," she says to me.

"Right?"

"It *is* her body."

Not in here, it's not, I want to say. Not anywhere, it's not, or not for long. She's a thing. I'm a thing. You're a thing, lying there, tubes feeding you, tubes draining you. You weren't sterilized by choice, were you? Not at your age. Some hotshot doctor must have decided you were deformed or malfunctioning or diseased. I don't say anything, trying not to let the anger or pity or whatever it is for us all make my hands shake. I have to be good with a needle, that's all.

"That stuff," she says, nodding to the needle, "gives me hallucinations."

"Yeah, it can. You'll only be on it for a couple of days. Then you won't need it."

"Need it?"

"For pain."

"Ah, pain."

I think she may want to argue about it, but she doesn't. I give her the shot, and then, instead of leaving her to it, I stand there, smooth the covers, and wipe her face as she begins to sweat.

"Every child I know is in here with broken bones," she says quietly, like a fact.

There's nothing to say about that. You don't contradict. It's too confusing. You don't go along either unless you're asked to. I hold her hand and wipe her face. Some faces simply clarify under strain. She has closed her eyes, almost as if it were a courtesy to me. Bobo does that sometimes, shy to trouble me, though she's so ready with questions most of the time. I don't usually think of Bobo while I'm working. I get this woman's hallucinations without drugs if I do, but this is different, companionable. I have never been confused before between who is comforter and who is comforted, except with Bobo. Am I going to start playing mother instead of nurse? I can't seem to feel the harm in it if there's time. The old woman has cried herself to sleep. The child calling is for the next station.

"Could you see if Bobby's all right?" she asks, opening her eyes, very dark with the drug now. "It's Bobby out there."

"Who's Bobby?" I ask.

"A child, just a child."

I let go of her hand and wait a minute. Then I say, "It's not Bobby."

"Thank you."

Or Bobo—a child, just a child. I can't think about that. I wipe her face again to comfort myself.

Later that night, when I had time, I looked at her record: Diana

Parks, thirty years old (two years older than I), single (still, Bobby could be her child), a teacher. The suspected cancer of her uterus wasn't there. I should have felt relieved, but there was a swell of irrational anger instead, as if her uterus had been ripped out of her for idle curiosity.

"It's *my* body." I saw again the sagging skin of that old woman's thighs, forced apart, the rape my own hand had almost attempted with the catheter, given up only for the noise it would make. A thing, just a thing, we all are. I couldn't know anything else, and yet I did because Diana Parks mattered to me.

Bobby was not Diana's child but one of the students she'd worried about leaving just as he had begun to respond, come up out of the apathy of surviving multiple burns. Diana taught children who had been injured or crippled, and she talked about each one not as a case but as a person. She would have sounded like a mother except for the singular detachment she had from guilt, either of having brought them into the world or having been helplessly responsible for what had happened to them. Sometimes, as she talked, I could feel impatience and envy for the free pleasure she took in those children, until I came upon the free pleasure and even pride I was taking in her as each night she was stronger, her incision healing quickly.

"I don't think they'll even be able to keep you around long enough to take the stitches out," I said.

"No, the doctor said this morning he'd get me home for Mother's Day," Diana said.

"For what?"

"I did laugh, and then he realized his mistake and was terribly embarrassed."

The anger in me was so intense I didn't dare speak. I turned away so that she couldn't read it in my face, but Diana caught my hand and turned me back to her.

"I don't mind. I never intended to have children of my own anyway. I was sorry I embarrassed him."

"I'd have killed him!"

"Nonsense, you would have wanted to get home for Mother's Day."

"For *you*," I said before I realized how that would sound, what it might mean.

"Why don't you come to see me instead and bring Bobo? I need to meet Bobo."

"It would be too soon. You really shouldn't even be looking after yourself for the first week."

"Oh, I won't be. I live with a friend."

I didn't take Bobo to meet Diana Parks on Mother's Day. I took her to the beach instead, to be out of the house all day. The box propped up against the door when we got back was not the flowers I dreaded from Bobo's father—he could still do things like that—but a present for Bobo, a string puppet from Diana, which said, "Happy child's day." I would have burned it, but Bobo was absolutely delighted with it, and I had to shake hands with it, watch it dance and bow all evening long, and answer Bobo's questions asked in a voice she'd invented for the puppet. "When can we see Diana? When? When? When?"

At first I thought they had both known and kept it as a bad joke on me, but then she was hugging me and laughing and saying, "Lee? Lee? Can it really be you?" And I realized she was just as surprised as I was.

"Do you know each other, then?" Diana was asking from a chair in their living room.

"We roomed together the first year of college," Bobo explained.

Then they both looked down at my daughter standing there quietly with her puppet in its box.

"She isn't exactly named for you." I said, embarrassed. "I had to name her Elizabeth for my mother-in-law. But I've always called her Bobo because she asks so many questions."

"Is your name Bobo?"

"It used to be," Bobo answered her namesake. "Most people call me Barbara now."

I turned to Diana, feeling the shock of love which for a week I had been trying to corrupt with jealousy for this unknown friend. It would have been easy to feel jealous of Diana for having found my kind and kinky Bobo, whom I must learn to call Barbara for clarity's sake. Anything but pleasure seemed very much beside the point.

Barbara was involved in educational research and wrote articles for both medical and educational journals. She liked her job, which took her around the country, posing questions to people, some of whom found her as baffling and comic as I had those years ago, as obvious and irrelevant: the planners for whom an idea just gets in the way. Diana, her lovely face intent on Barbara whenever she spoke, was obviously not a planner and had never been.

"Do you understand now?" I had to ask.

Barbara shook her head and laughed. She was getting other puppets out for Bobo. They were going to the kitchen to make up a play for Diana and me.

"Why didn't you come last Sunday?" Diana asked as soon as they had left the room.

"I had thought you lived alone. I was jealous, I guess. Silly."

"Yes, waiting a week to find you have two friends instead of one."

"How long have you and Bobo — Barbara — lived together?"

"Five years."

It was awkward. I had touched her so intimately through those nights in the hospital, my hands so functional I did not need excuses. Now I didn't have an excuse, a clear reason instead never to touch her again. I didn't know what words to throw across that gap.

Bobo and Barbara came back into the room with three puppets.

"This is a story about friends," Bobo explained, "old friends and new friends."

She consulted Barbara and then announced, "Old friends hug and kiss and laugh and ask each other questions."

Bobo's puppet and one of Barbara's went through that exercise with much stilted violence while Bobo imitated me and Barbara imitated herself. "Lee? Lee? Can it really be you?"

Then Bobo announced, "New friends are shy."

Her puppet and Barbara's other puppet sat down a good distance from each other, bowed their heads to each other and waved.

Diana and I both laughed, and then Diana said, "But where are you in all this, Bobo?"

"Oh," Bobo said, "I'm just me."

Still too young to be yanked around on the strings of convention, to see it all instead as a show for your entertainment. Oh, Bobo, darling, why do you have to grow up? Couldn't I grow down instead? In and down, to find the person of my flesh I first discovered in you.

Diana was right. I had suddenly two friends instead of one. At first Diana and Barbara talked about their work while I listened. I had always thought of the hospital as something to be shut out and forgotten the moment my shift was over. I had hated the way my husband talked about his work, the callous and gross jokes he told, though I was supposed to understand that it was a healthy attitude for a man who had to deal with the sick and dying. Diana and Barbara talked about the doctors they worked with as if they were human beings; and there didn't seem to be many working with children who were impatient, mechanical bullies. Some were too rigid. Some jumped too easily to new conclusions, but most of them seemed to take time to listen to Diana's observations about her children, to read Barbara's articles. The man in white with mysterious powers, a Mercedes, and a set of golf clubs whom I had married was not every doctor in the hospital; nor was I, as I began to watch others, every nurse. I was changing, not at first because I wanted to. I had realized when I went back to work that I was always looking for a place to deposit my anger, finding nearly every decision made by a doctor stupid and insensitive. Now I had to have some place to use up the tenderness I felt for Diana. The hands I held, the faces I wiped, the hallucinations I became party to were all really hers. But in a need to share my work with Barbara and Diana, I began to pay some real attention to the persons in the flesh I tended.

Sometimes Bobo and I had dinner with Diana and Barbara, and then Bobo spent the night with them. I'd pick her up in the morning when I'd finished my shift. Barbara had usually gone to work. Diana would have a meal waiting for me, and I'd have that hour with her before I took Bobo to play school and went home for a few hours' sleep.

The first time Barbara went away, fondly instructing me to look after Diana, who was back at work herself by then, I was terrified. I wouldn't go to their apartment for dinner; and if Diana came to us, I kept Bobo up until she had gone home. Bobo was a willing enough chaperone, but one night she simply fell asleep in Diana's lap.

"Poor baby," Diana said, looking down at her. "We've worn her out with our games. Put her to bed."

When I came back into the room to confront that lovely, concerned face, I was shaking.

"Come here, Lee," she said, "please."

"Barbara's my oldest friend," I said, as I went to her. "She always wanted to understand. I thought it was a joke. I could have loved her, Diana. I try to think about her." I was holding both Diana's hands for the first time since she'd left the hospital, but I was hanging onto them now against my own hallucinations. "My husband—he had other women. It made me feel like a thing. I don't think I knew what it was to feel human, except with Bobo, until I met both of you. Do you know, I touch all my patients now the way I touched you, as if I really cared? And I really do care, and instead of tearing me apart, it's begun to put me together."

Diana was holding me very quietly. "She does understand. Can't you?"

I couldn't. But I couldn't stop either, open to a need for joy as if it were a gasp for breath, and now I could hear that old woman crying, "It's my body. It's my body," but not in struggle—in wonder, and it was my voice, amazed.

You don't stop being a planner and turn into a thinker overnight. Barbara might understand my love for Diana and hers for me, but I wanted to organize it, for her convenience as well as our own. What that meant at first was lying about it, but Diana wouldn't hear of that. She wouldn't even lie to Bobo, for whom our demonstrations of affection obviously seemed a lot more natural than my nervous distance of the weeks before had been. "Old friends hug and kiss and laugh and ask each other questions." So many questions. All right, loving did not have to be a tragedy. Even my husband's having other women was not a tragedy, except in *having* at all. It's my body, and it's your body, and it's her body. We are persons, not things. All right. But no one can be more than one place at a time. I would be very generous. I felt generous. "Will you promise me you'll never be with me if Barbara needs you? Will you promise me you'll never be with me unless you want to be?" Of course not, Diana said. One of her children had died in the toilet while she was running bases for a wheelchair ball game on the playground. "What does that have to do with us?" Everything. We all have jobs. We all have other commitments. "But doesn't Barbara have to come first?" Diana's face, intent and kind, was tired. I didn't want to go on being frantic and ridiculous. I didn't even want to try to understand. I wanted to love her, as I did love her.

Barbara came home. How I envied Bobo's simple shout of plea-sure as she hurled herself into Barbara's arms. I stood back, still a puppet on strings, by now not even able to act out the pantomime of old friends. I had another script to get through: guilt, and then jeal-ousy. Barbara, kind, kinky Barbara, for whom I'd named my daughter as much as I dared, how could I be jealous of her? But I was. That she refused to be jealous of me only made it worse.

I so badly needed to be with Diana that I accepted Barbara's fre-quent offers to entertain Bobo, though I felt both obligated and re-sentful. One night, after they had a particularly happy day at the beach, Bobo said, "I wish babies were made with two mothers. Then BigBo could be my mother, too." From that moment, I was con-vinced Barbara, in the guise of kindness, was taking Bobo from me in revenge. I couldn't, even with panic as inspiration, stop seeing Diana immediately and therefore separate Bobo and Barbara. Bobo wouldn't have understood it, and if I was frightened of losing her to Barbara, I was as terrified of losing her because of Barbara. Against the impulse to love, mine for Diana, Bobo's for Barbara, I had to plan a defense, a slow and careful withdrawal nobody would notice until it was ac-complished.

In a month, I had reduced the time the four of us spent together by nearly half without having to confront Bobo with too many disap-pointments, without running out of credible excuses for Diana and Barbara, who were both really very easy to deceive. When Barbara went off on another business trip, I couldn't resist the temptation to see Diana again every day, telling myself that, when Barbara came back, I could use the excuse of giving them time to themselves to withdraw again. But Bobo did not want to be with Diana as often as I did; and when we were three together, she whined or sulked, flip-pant with our attention, angry without it. Diana was more patient with her than I was.

"Let's make a play about missing BigBo," Diana suggested.

"I won't!" Bobo shouted. "I don't care!"

"Bobo!" I shouted back.

She ran into her room and slammed the door.

"She can be just as cold as her damned father!" I said, tears contracting in my throat. "She's just jealous."

"Then we have to teach her not to be," Diana said quietly. "She is missing Barbara."

"*You're* missing Barbara."

"Of course I am . . . "

"And always reminding Bobo, 'Let's make a play about missing Big-Bo!' " I heard and hated the simper in my voice, but I went right on. "That's how you take care of the guilt, isn't it? Give Bobo to Barbara and it's an even trade. Well, it won't work. Bobo's *mine.*"

"Lee . . . Lee . . . " It was a call more than a reprimand, but I didn't listen to it.

"It's sick," I said. "The whole thing's sick. It's not a triangle; it's a square . . . and with a child. I used to think *wife*-swapping would be horrible."

In the silence after Diana left, I could hear Bobo crying. I wanted to go in to her, to hold her in my arms, to tell her it was all right now. I'd never do anything so crazy again, never frighten her or make her jealous. But I couldn't. Her tears weren't for me. They were for BigBo. I stood outside her door, wanting to shout what would be insanities to a five-year-old, things like, "If I give up Diana, you can give up BigBo. It's even-Steven, okay?" Instead, I just put my head against the door and remembered shouting, "She can be just as cold as her damned father!" Was I going to begin hating Bobo, too? I didn't have to love anyone else, ever. I didn't want to. I didn't know how. "You'll forget her, Bobo," I wanted to say, but what if she did? Next, it would probably be her first-grade teacher, no swaps involved, me with no place in it at all.

"Bobo?" I opened the door. She was lying on her bed, her face in her pillow. She let me touch her, but she kept her face turned away. I began to rub her back, and gradually the sobs turned to deep, trembling sighs. "Would you like a glass of milk?" She nodded into her pillow. While I was getting it, I heard her go to the bathroom and wash her face. She came out very dignified, sat next to me on the couch, and asked to be read to, letting me be kind to her while she settled her grief out of my way. As Diana had once, closing her eyes against her pain to spare me the sight of it, reminded me of Bobo, now Bobo reminded me of Diana, and the pain was brutal.

I just can't go on shouting, "I don't care!" teaching Bobo that's the only way to deal with hurt. It's time this grotesque puppet show was over. It's time for BigBo to come home. She understands, and I've simply got to, even when it hurts, just close my eyes for a minute. It's my body; it's my pain. I can't plan my way out of it. My life depends on it.

Outlander

AT THE SANATORIUM, where she had been committed the year before by her family, Ann Bacon was told she had a fifty-fifty chance,
with luck and help and courage. Her age was against her. She was
forty-nine. But her anger might help her. She did not want to go
home again to the righteous indignation of her sober friends and family. They had taken what was left of her inheritance and put it in involuntary trust for her three children. The income was enough for
her to live on anywhere but at home in that city of clubs and ser-
vants and French underwear. She had never had enough money,
widowed when the children were hardly out of diapers, dependent
on her rich father's stern charity until the children were grown and
educated and he died, leaving her suddenly free and alone. She was
drinking before that, but she was protected, first by her youngest
daughter until she went away to college, then by Fran O'Connell, a
young schoolteacher who came to live with her. But once her father
was dead and the money was hers, she didn't care about protection.
At first the children came home to try to reason and bully her into
health, but she only drank herself into a deaf rage. Then her friends
stopped opening the door to her, and finally her sister's husband
threatened to commit her. The only person who did not lecture or
threaten was Fran O'Connell, who perhaps did not think it was her
place to, simply a boarder in the house, and who perhaps also understood why Ann Bacon drank, listening so often to the fury only
one glass of gin could release in her. Ann Bacon had never wanted to
be the dependent fool death had made of her. For her children's sake
she had endured it. They were grown and settled. The old tyrant
was dead. She would take room for her anger, which was all that
was left of her pride. But threatened with committal, she was afraid.
She drank all night and in the morning bought a plane ticket to South
America. She drove toward the airport at a speed that would leave a

whole city of pursuers behind her. She was found in a field, thrown clear of her overturned car. She'd had a fifty-fifty chance then, and she'd lived. She had a fifty-fifty chance now, and she wanted it.

Fran O'Connell, who had been in no position to argue against either the committal or the involuntary trust, could and did write to Ann Bacon all through that long year and came to visit her occasionally, proud of her progress, proud of her fighting will. A gentle, even fearful girl herself, she saw in Ann Bacon not a self-indulgent, menopausal drunk but a brave woman in a passionate struggle to be free. She admired Ann and loved her as she would have liked to love a mother if she'd had one. But Fran herself was not a child, nearly thirty. She had become, therefore, Ann's friend.

It was Fran O'Connell who waited for Ann Bacon, offering her the help she would need. They went to Boston and lived there through an uncertain winter; for Ann, alone during the day, hadn't enough to do. She enjoyed reading; and at the sanatorium, where it was understood that therapy for women should be carpentry, for men fine handcrafts, Ann had learned to work with wood. But more than a book a day only cluttered her mind, and after she had made a fine inlaid frame for a mirror, she saw no point in it. Fran suggested that she take a course in something, but Ann was shy of her finishing-school education, the long gap of years in her mind. And the city itself oppressed her, heavy with all she admired in Henry James and hated of the world he knew. Often on weekends, they drove out of the city, east and then north into New Hampshire and Vermont. Always as they drove into that winter landscape of white birches in the snow, Ann was happy. Always, as they drove back toward the city, she could feel the tension of old angers. The third time she got drunk, she smashed the mirror and severed the tendon in her left thumb.

"What are we going to do?" Fran asked simply.

"Get out of here," Ann said. "That's what we're going to do. We're going to go live in the country."

In that hope, Ann stayed sober through the week for the trip they would take on the weekend, searching for the place they could live. In that early spring, through thaw and mud time, they drove the nearly impassable back roads, until one May Saturday, at the edge of a New Hampshire township that numbered seven hundred and fifty souls, they found The Fork, a twenty-acre farm with a four-room farmhouse that had stood on the land since the arrival of the early settlers. It had neither plumbing nor electricity. A false ceiling had closed in its hand-hewn beams, and a dozen wallpapers covered the pine walls, but they were there under the catalogue taste of generations of farmers' wives. The sliding shutters were still there for protection against Indian arrows; and the rooms themselves were ample, with large fireplaces opening off the central chimney. Next to the house was a barn. Both before and behind the house and barn the land fell away, to woods at the back, to a meadow at the front.

"I don't suppose we could live in it in the winter," Fran said.

"No . . . but as a summer place, and perhaps later on we could fix it up."

Ann Bacon phoned her banker brother-in-law, speaking to him for the first time since she had been committed, and he agreed to advance her the money to buy the place.

In June the two women moved in, and they hadn't been there more than three weeks before Ann's children began to arrive. The loft of the barn was turned into a dormitory, filled with cots and sleeping bags. There wasn't enough water from the one well. Ann's son spoke to the man at the general store, who gave him the country solution: well water's for drinking, not washing in. There was plenty of advice like that for each problem. What they didn't have they got along without. Ann, who had nearly forgotten how to cook, learned again on a wood stove. Fran worked to get in a late garden. Ann's son and son-in-law decided to build a stone terrace out in front under the big trees. Ann's daughter bought a horse at an auction. Someone was always chopping wood and hauling water. All through July and August The Fork endured these outlanders, these city slickers, who turned hard, mostly silly work into holiday.

As the last of her children, her youngest, packed her car and got ready to leave, she said happily, "You're so well, Mother, you're not even going to need Fran much longer."

"What did she mean by that?" Ann demanded in the first evening they should have sat quietly by their own hearth.

Fran, thinking Ann had been told more than she had, admitted that Ann's brother-in-law had offered Fran money, a kind of salary to stay with Ann.

"But I refused it," Fran said. "I told him it wasn't a matter of money . . ."

Ann got up and started toward the door.

"Ann, wait a minute," Fran said, not pleading, very quiet. "If you go, I'm not coming after you."

"Not even if you're paid to?" Ann asked sarcastically.

"If you go," Fran said again, "I'm not coming after you . . . ever."

Ann stood, caught by an anger which was pride. Then she walked back to her chair and sat down. For a long time neither of them spoke.

"I can't go back," Ann said finally. "Will you stay with me here . . . through the winter?"

"How can we?" Fran asked.

"People have," Ann said.

She was fifty years old, and Fran was thirty. They knew nothing of country ways or country people except what they had discovered that summer and laughed about among themselves and Ann's city children, who had left them prepared for the winter with a stone terrace and a horse.

"I suppose I could get a job," Fran said.

"I chop wood better than any of the others," Ann said, and it was true.

"But we'll have to have friends to help us . . ."

"Friends," Ann repeated, a word that had seemed to her foreign since her young womanhood.

"We'll go to church first of all," Fran said.

"I'm a Presbyterian," Ann said.

"Not anymore. From now on you're a Congregationalist. And there's no problem about that. You like to vote. You'd even like God to stand for re-election now and then."

Ann smiled. God, when she was angry with Him, looked very like her father. Ann, when she smiled, looked very like him, too. She had a handsome face, which had lined early, recording not dissipation but struggle, pride, will. She was tan from the summer, and her eyes were clear and warm in the firelight, in hope. She was strong-bodied, shrewd in the use of physical strength, her hands articulate. And, yes, she could be a Congregationalist if she had to. She felt she could be almost anything, if she had to, to survive this winter here at The Fork, at home.

Fran, who was neither strong nor intelligent-bodied, who had neither the need nor the will to set herself impossible tests of survival, had only one thing to sustain her: her faith in Ann's will, which was also love. That would have to do.

When Ann announced at the general store that they intended to stay the winter, she met nothing but skeptical silence. A couple of fool women and their relatives holidaying at The Fork for the summer was one thing; a couple of fool women in the winter was another. It would be as much nuisance as the town's taking on another whole family of Caws, who were numerous and good for nothing except getting drunk or sick or both; and the town already had all it could do to keep the young ones from starving or going to jail, the old ones from freezing. But the most open objection came to Ann from the farmer across the road, who said only, "Gets pretty cold up here in the winter." What else could a man say to such foolishness? Later the doctor reassured him with, "They'll be gone with the first snow. Don't worry about it."

There was no job for Fran at the two-room school until in mid-October one of the teachers died. "Well, if they can need one of us . . ." said Ann, who was already discouraged about making friends with anybody, in church or out of it. Every time she tried to strike up a conversation with one of the men about anything practical, he shut up as tight as a bank on Sunday. Reasoning that they were all afraid of being used, she made a few friendly, political remarks only to discover that she and Fran and the minister were the only Democrats for miles. She would have liked to settle to talk with the minister, with that in common, but she was still shy about her new voting privileges in church, afraid her Presbyterian slip was showing.

"No singing or drawing or any of those other idlenesses," Fran reported. "What they want to know is how to read the catalogue and count every penny."

While Fran was at school, Ann suffered no sense of too little to do. She was cutting some of her own trees, using the horse to drag the logs up to the barn, splitting wood to make a pile as high as the house, which still wouldn't last the winter as she tried to calculate it. Once the cold set in, they'd live in the kitchen and bedroom. Even then, unless she did something to insulate the rooms better, they'd be apt to freeze to death sitting right in front of the fire. Now that Fran was teaching, they didn't worry so much about being snowed in. The town would plow The Fork road to see its teacher got to school. Still there should be stores in the cellar, of food, of fuel for the lamps. And what about water?

When the first snow came, the doctor's prediction was wrong. The general store was treated to a visit from Mrs. Bacon and Miss O'Connell, riding in their horse-drawn sleigh, looking as cheery as a Christmas card.

But after the second snow, after the third, when the walk between the house and barn was shoulder-deep, and the temperature began to drop, they faced the real hazards of a primitive winter.

"Things freeze here I just didn't think about freezing," Ann said to the general storekeeper. "When you find your own front door frozen shut . . ."

But they didn't ask for help until two days before Christmas, when part of the roof caved in under the load of snow and ice. Actually it was a relief to the men in the town to come to their aid, both because they could finally have a cause for all the grumbling they'd done and because you couldn't really be neighborly with anyone until they owed you something.

For all the terrors of winter, mud season, which they'd known only as weekend tourists before, was what nearly broke their determination. There were days when neither the car nor the horse could make it out over the road, and there was nothing to do but wait without belief that the muck could ever harden again into a passable surface.

"My God, how I've learned to hate spring!" Ann sighed.

But only two weeks later she filled her lungs with the first fragrance of growing things and said, "God's own sweet air!"

Looking back on that winter, as she often did, Ann would say, "Oh, we got help, all right, whenever we needed it. What we didn't get was encouragement, not one word of encouragement."

When the summer came, there was no more nonsense about stone terraces.

"We've got to get a furnace into the house and insulate it properly and bring in electricity, and solve the water problem," Ann announced to her children. "Last winter we didn't know any better. This winter we'd be crazy."

One day, one of the boys brought home a cow. Everyone stood around, very interested in it, though they were more accustomed to kicking tires in making appraisals of things that size.

"Does anybody know how to milk one?" Fran asked, always the timid and practical one.

"You just . . . milk it," Ann said, with an inappropriate but confident gesture.

But nobody could, and the poor creature, suffering at the hands of more and more exasperated amateurs, was in obvious pain.

"You children will be the death of me," Ann announced as she strode off down the road to old Mr. Jordan, who lived with his wife in a cottage at the corner.

"Don't nobody know how to milk a cow," he was still repeating as he arrived to give the needed lesson. But then he looked at the cow and felt her. "This cow ain't goin' to let her milk down to nobody for a while now."

She turned out to be the hardest milker in two counties, but Ann learned just the same. The secret she confided only to her family. "Presbyterian hymns. Apparently cows are Presbyterian."

Something soft and amused was coming into the aging of that handsome face.

Power and heat were expensive but possible. Water was not. They had to wait another year to buy old Jordan's house when his wife died and he went to a daughter's to live. On his ten acres was the spring that could supply their needs amply. They would have a bathroom.

"I don't know that I remember how to behave in one," Fran said, but she hadn't become as much of a country girl as that; the first time the cow had to be serviced by a bull, she thought they had to spend the night together.

Even there, so much cut off from the world, the news of the war concerned everyone increasingly. Nobody, good isolationist Republicans that they all were, believed for a minute that the United States should get into it any more than they believed England could ever be defeated. Still, it worried at people, like a distant weather.

When Ann's son came to tell her that he was going to Canada to join the RCAF, she could not try to discourage him. Patriotism was not only the love of a landscape, a land, but its traditions and its principles, both of which were being challenged in Europe. Oh, and the dangerous heroism appealed to her, the laying down a life for what one believed. Part of Ann's grief was the prison of passivity her womanhood had locked her into, the unseemliness for her of fighting for anything with all the angry energy and physical strength she had. She envied her son and blessed him. His wife and son would come to live at The Fork.

That necessity gave Ann the argument she needed for enough money to put two bedrooms and a bath in the attic of the farmhouse. Her banker brother-in-law could not refuse. Ann did not really know how much money she did have at her disposal. She knew that income was held back "for emergencies" so that there was always a reserve. Legally she had signed away the right to draw on it without her brother-in-law's permission. In some instances, her children's signatures were required as well. She was too humiliated to shout a sober anger at Fran. She drank for three days instead, free then to shout anything that occurred to her, a hero imprisoned in her sex, deprived of the right to kill German or brother-in-law, exiled to this stony New England farm, in a Republican jail with a timid, moralizing, prim little jailkeeper who, for all she knew, was being paid for the job. On the third night, Fran did not come home.

Ann, drunken, bull-angry, and terrified, stumbled into the town to find her, shouting lunatic threats at the quiet white houses set back from the square. The minister's wife went out to fetch her.

"What does your house know about a Presbyterian hell?" Ann demanded, but she went, stumbling and cursing, into what was at least a Democratic study, where Fran sat with the minister. "I will not be chastened!"

The man she would have so liked for a friend laughed.

"Sobered then," he said. "That's all that's necessary."

"Or humored or prayed over or committed!"

"Those are your own jobs to do," the minister said.

"So much for an elected representative for salvation," Ann said. She sat down heavily. "Ah, I'm such an old fool, Fran. Come home and help me clean the place up."

The next morning she phoned her brother-in-law, who offered no opposition. He even suggested that he and her sister would like someday to be invited to The Fork. "Any cold day in hell," Ann would have liked to reply, but her anger was temporarily spent, and she had what she wanted.

There were no professional builders in the neighborhood. For any project that was beyond one man's skill or strength, others worked in the hours they could spare from their own farms. The general store-keeper was the best electrician and could come only at night unless somebody else had a day to take over the store. Labor was sometimes paid for, more often traded for a carload of manure or the loan of a tractor or a day's work at harvesting time. Ann Bacon still had not much to offer in that sort of bargaining, but surprisingly Fran O'Connell did. The carpenter's little girl wanted piano lessons, and the storekeeper's son was having trouble with his high school math course. Ann was proud that they did not have to pay in the way of city people, but she wished she had more of her own to offer. It wasn't likely that anyone would call on a woman in her fifties to help with a barn-raising, though she was as canny as most of the men when it came to that sort of thing. Because it was her own place, the men certainly couldn't stop her from doing some of the work herself, however. Gradually the talk at a lot of supper tables was about Mrs. Bacon's way with a level and plane. And if it was a bit queer that she talked to it and sang to it while she worked, the wood did understand what she wanted of it. That they could see. If there was a lot of narrow prejudice in those farming people, still they would believe what they could see. It wasn't a farm those two women ran, mind you, not with a swaybacked riding horse and a tight-titted cow, their fields let out to John Gange across the road for grazing his young stock, in trade for manure for their garden in the spring. Still, they kept their fences mended and asked no more than they were willing to give. And Mrs. Bacon made the best potato salad and the second-best berry pie at a church supper. Contrary to their first fears about

Miss O'Connell, she didn't give airs to any of the youngsters who wouldn't have had them anyway. They did want two bathrooms in a house where only four people were going to live, but everybody had peculiarities. You didn't have to look far past your own family to know that. Some had a hard time not knowing it under their own roofs.

So by the end of summer, the house was ready for a daughter-in-law and a grandson. Ann felt sure the land could teach a boy nearly all that a father could; and she had, after all, raised a son herself, one to be proud of. But her daughter-in-law, a city girl, would be lonely. The friends Ann could not bring herself to make for herself or for Fran she began to make for her daughter-in-law. The minister and his wife came to dinner and talked politics with an appetite and sanity Ann had loved at her father's table, for, however personally pigheaded he had been, he was a man of national good sense. For their guests, too, it was a glad release. Fran brought home the other schoolteacher, a prissy little old maid who had read more books than Ann had heard of and promised to lend her some. The young couple renting old Jordan's house began to spend some evenings with them. He was writing a thesis on reforestation, but what he loved to talk about was how a farm like this could be worked again; and, because he was not a farmer, he was willing to tell Ann facts her farming neighbors considered good trade secrets. It was not a wide world of people, but it was a warm and lively one by the time they welcomed Joyce and Timmy in the early fall.

That December the United States was at war. And before six months had passed, there was not an able-bodied young man left in the town or county.

"You'd have thought, the way they talk, Republicans would have waited for the draft," Ann said to the minister, and they smiled together, in more pride than amusement at their neighbors.

Whatever reserve there might have been at allowing Mrs. Bacon and Miss O'Connell into the community as full members with a right to a place at the table or at the sickbed or in the barn or in the field fell away now in the greater need of the community for every person in it. Aside from a Caw or two, either waiting for the draft or plotting minor maimings to avoid it, no young men were left for young men's jobs. The older men took those on, leaving some of their traditional tasks to the women. If Mrs. Bacon could hang a door straight, let her hang it. If Miss O'Connell could educate a stubborn pump as well as a stubborn child, let her go ahead and educate. Young Mrs. Bacon turned up in the doctor's office as his receptionist so that the doctor's wife, who was a trained nurse, could help with the rounds. Though at first Joyce made a few mistakes about whether or not a pig was a fair trade for a gallbladder, she soon got the gist of it. People helped her, since, in a national emergency, keeping those sorts of secrets from city people didn't seem as important. There were realer, stranger enemies to consider.

Ann made what at first seemed the bad mistake of introducing one of those enemies to the town. Having lost her tenants in the old Jordan house and seeing not much chance, in these days, of renting it again, she decided, having read about the number of displaced persons coming into the country, to offer the house to such a refugee family. She asked for farmers. They arrived one night, a tubercular and broken man with his huge, hardy wife. They spoke no word of English; they were Poles with some German. Before they had been installed for forty-eight hours, rumor went round that Mrs. Bacon was harboring spies.

The minister did his best. He preached a sermon about the plight of these people, encouraging others to join Mrs. Bacon and Miss O'Connell in Christian charity and practical good sense. These were people who were willing to work, and the community needed them. But they spoke a language that sounded to the farmers like nothing but Hitler's own ranting. In the first week, someone set fire to their shed. Then their water pipe was disconnected. Ann didn't believe these acts of vandalism were the work of any of her farmer neighbors. She was convinced one Caw or another was using people as an excuse to stir up trouble. One night she caught young Jay Caw hanging around near her own barn, and she chased him off the property with her squirrel gun. But the incidents, instead of arousing sympathy, seemed to increase suspicion. Every time now anything happened, whether small theft or a marked increase in mastitis in the cows, her refugees were blamed. Caws, who had always been called thieves but never had been given the status of witches, didn't know whether to resent or enjoy the new innocence assigned to them. Even without community resentment, Ann and Fran faced trouble of their own with their not very well thought out charity. First, they couldn't talk sensibly with either man or woman. Second, they really hadn't planned exactly what either would do. Ann had decided it was time to work their land, get a small herd of cows, some chickens, perhaps even some pigs, though both Fran and Joyce were adamant about not having pigs. They were not enthusiastic about the responsibility of any more animals. The house was already overrun with the runts of litters of barn cats, one of which was blind and kept bumping into the furniture. But Ann argued that a displaced farmer could teach them all they needed to know and take much of the responsibility of the work for himself. Before a month had passed, it was obvious that their farmer was neither willing nor capable. Whatever chore could be made clear to them as their responsibility the wife agreed to and did. He simply sat by the stove and waited to die.

"Nevertheless," Ann announced at the dinner table, "this is a national emergency. This farm has got to produce. You've got your teaching to do, Fran, and Joyce is busy at the office, but I'm free, and I can't really get those two back to work until there's real work to do."

Their own barn, half storage and garage, wasn't big enough for more than another couple of cows, but the loft could be heated for chickens, and the barn on the old Jordan place, with fixing up, could be used for the cows.

"But what if you got sick?" Fran asked.

"I'll help you, Granny," Timmy said.

"Chasing chickens!" Joyce replied.

"I could chase chickens," he agreed.

Within three months, they had a herd of eight cows, Ann buying cheaply the hard milkers she had learned to understand. By now, other farmers called her instead of the vet when a cow was freshening with too much reluctance. And if she sang, nobody objected to it. Then came the chickens; and as these arrived, the man by the stove finally got up and went to tend them. He could speak to them in his native tongue and be as well understood as he had been by his cows and chickens at home. His wife gradually learned enough English to help with the planning of a much larger vegetable garden, a "victory" garden.

"We will fight with vegetables," she announced, pleased that she understood.

He would never learn. The best he could do was to struggle up to the house calling, "Bacon, Bacon, cow *krank*," holding himself where his udders would have been, and such efforts were reserved for extreme emergencies.

Still, he was willing to live. Ann was satisfied with him for that; and if the rest of the community didn't accept her Poles, gradually they learned to ignore them.

The crisis of the year came not from any of the ambitious undertakings of the farm but from the request of Ann's youngest daughter to marry a young officer about to go overseas. She wanted a small wedding at home, which would include Ann's sister and brother-in-law.

"If you don't want them, tell her so," Fran said.

"It's her wedding," Ann answered, her back turned.

"It's *our* house."

Ann took a pack of cigarettes from her shirt pocket and struck a kitchen match on the seat of her blue jeans. Then she went out the back door and walked down the road, noticing her fence-patching with pleasure, smelling God's own sweet air, which was stronger now with the animal smells of her working farm.

"But it's her home," Ann said aloud. She knew that, if she refused, this youngest daughter would feel free to do what she would probably prefer: marry among friends in the house of her aunt and uncle, from whom she had often fiercely protected her mother but in whom she had found a security Ann had not given her.

"They've been very good to her," Ann said after her walk, knowing that Fran's objection was not based on her own anger but on the anger she feared in Ann. Therefore, she did not add what she dreadfully felt: that this was at last the cold day in hell she had promised her sister and brother-in-law.

How could she expect their city eyes to see in the beams and warm wood of the living room the months of work that had gone into stripping off the layers and layers of old paper? How could they feel the winter nights of sanding and oiling that had gone into the arms of the chairs they sat in, country antiques she had bought at auctions with a good eye for line? What could they know of the luxury of warmth, of running water, of jars of vegetables from her own garden lined on shelves she had built herself? They would see nothing but the quaint, impractical farmhouse, where cats couldn't always be trusted not to use the ashes in the fireplaces, where chickens occasionally strayed into the kitchen, where a little boy with scabs on knees and elbows, a bowl haircut, was growing up with a country boy's grammar and manners, knowing more about the sexual and excretory practices of animals than his great aunt yet knew about the human body, and willing to tell her so. And what would they see in Ann's face, then years-aged by the hard New England weather, but the alcoholic ruin they wanted to see? She still looked as smart as anyone, in her Sunday suit, going off to church, but what would she wear for her daughter's wedding: silk her horny hands would tear before she'd got it over her head, forgotten diamonds on a finger whose blue nail would not fall off for another two months? A bare-armed country woman with a farmer's tan, white hair cropped for forking hay and shoveling manure. Oh, they would see something of the hard work, all right; and they would call it her punishing salvation. Damn them! Damn them both!

But Ann wrote to her daughter and agreed, and the plans for the wedding were made.

Ann's temper, her curse and her strength, was always shortest on weekends when Fran and Joyce and Timmy were underfoot continually, particularly in the winter and in the stormy days of spring when Timmy was not tempted into the out-of-doors to work off his child's energy. Still, she rarely scolded him directly. She would grumble to Fran about a blocked pump, to Joyce about an empty can of oil left on the shelf. The young women endured in shared sympathy until one of them, usually Joyce, would say to Timmy with real impatience, "Oh, go out and play. A little weather never hurt anyone." He would wait for a reprieve from his grandmother, for often she would relent; but one rainy spring Saturday he had to sulk out into the open in his boots and sou'wester. The house settled to a nervy quiet, which was possible. He was gone for over three hours and finally had to be called in to his dinner. Joyce looked at his eyes, wondering if he had a fever, but he seemed in high spirits, having forgotten his afternoon had been a punishment. When Ann went out to collect eggs from several hundred chickens, she found only three. Puzzled, she walked round the barn and found the wall away from the house entirely egg yolk yellow, glistening with a transparent glaze, occasionally broken by the sharp white shards of shells.

"Timmy!" she shouted, turning toward the house. "Timmy!"

He stood in his pajamas, rigid.

"Why did you do such a thing?" Ann demanded, still more awed than angered by what she had seen.

"Because it was fun," he answered.

Ann looked at him, her own grandson with those family-warm and defiant eyes, and the laughter in her burst over him like the spring rain.

"But he has to be punished," Joyce protested. "There must have been at least two hundred eggs!"

"Think of it!" Ann said, shaking her head in wonder. "What a three hours that must have been."

She herself had never given in to the temptation unless she found a range egg whose age she couldn't judge. Then she had the delight of shying it at the nearest tree, proud of her aim but happier still at the simple smashing. Two hundred of them! She lived on that vicarious relief for a week, never mind the mess and the explanations she had to make on her egg route.

Still, the tension in the house grew as the wedding date approached. There had to be a trip into Hanover to find all of them appropriate clothes, on which Ann insisted they must spend real money. She'd have no compromise in taste. For Joyce there was no problem. She was the size twelve every dress had been designed for. Ann, though she felt violent at her own image in the mirror, when it appeared in soft prints, did finally find a dress she was proud of. For Fran, who was shaped like a thin winter pear, the problem couldn't be handsomely solved, but she endured Ann's pulling and plucking at each thing she put on as if the dress rather than the flesh were to blame and finally made an arbitrary choice.

Fran and Joyce both felt hopeful that Ann would get through the day without drinking. Fran counted on the two sober years that had passed since the house had been remodeled. Joyce knew that Timmy's presence had more than once derailed Ann's need. Ann herself seemed determined to have the day exactly as her daughter wanted it.

The house was filled with flowering branches. The minister was there early, more friend than official, and helped to welcome the few neighbors and out-of-town guests who were arriving, using the front door, which was not opened more than half-a-dozen times a year. Ann chatted with the groom's parents and his sister, all of whom she liked immediately because they exclaimed over the house, its charm and its warmth, the work that must have gone into it to make it so very comfortable as well. Then she turned and saw her sister, dressed in an expensive tweed suit, shock and alarm closing quickly out of her eyes.

"Sarah," Ann said and moved to her at once, arms open, heart unaccountably open to this sister she had not seen in ten years.

She even found it easy enough to offer hands to her brother-in-law, thinner-haired, heavier, with even more mannerisms than she had remembered. For the monster she had made of him all these years, he seemed almost smaller than life-size, neither of them anything to fear, not on this day when her youngest and hardest-tested had come home to marry a fine, strong-faced, tender-eyed boy in uniform.

Fran played the wedding march on the piano in the book room, which had been their only room, except for the kitchen, in the first winter. The service was brief and happy, champagne and cake waiting in the dining room. Ann did not take anything to drink, though she felt on this day she could have without danger. She did not want her daughter or Fran to have one moment's anxiety on her account.

As she watched her sister's stiff self-consciousness, her brother-in-law's sweating nerves, neither of them at ease with her country neighbors or her daughter's new family, she remembered with a new pity the competitive social graces she had been raised to, where to make a mistake in dress was to be shamed or to give offense, where no one owed anyone else anything but an invitation to a cocktail party or interest on a mortgage. She owed John Gange, standing there resigned in his Sunday suit and silence, a solid roof in the dead of winter, a carload of manure every spring, and he owed her the cooking for his whole family when his wife was laid up, two deliveries of calves when they couldn't locate the vet, grazing space for his young stock; there was no end to either list and wouldn't be, never mind about politics. Most of the people in this room were in more debt and credit to each other than that nervous banker could ever understand. And no woman in the room would be looking at Sarah's suit with anything but admiration. Even Ann, who had so angrily tried to dress for her sister, realized that her sister had tried to dress for her, for a simple country wedding. If this meeting would not achieve the reconciliation Ann knew her daughter hoped for, it would at last end the old envy Ann had suffered for her sister's money, security, social position. Ann wondered suddenly if she would have been even angrier with such things than she had been without them, if the hard humiliation of her father's charity had not given her some way to fight free into the human debt and credit she now lived in. Fran smiled to her from across the room. Ann's gratitude was much deeper than her knowledge of all Fran had done to keep her alive, to give her hope. Fran loved her.

After the bride and groom left, the out-of-town guests were invited to the minister's house for dinner. At this house, no alcohol was ever served, and Ann realized that for her sister and brother-in-law this would make the final hours difficult, for they were both habitual drinkers of an anesthetic sort. What released in her all the bitterness of her life soothed them to a companionable stupidity with each other and their friends. She had first learned to drink in her sister's living room at a time when she wouldn't have dreamed of affording liquor of her own. Then she had thought her anger rose against the smug complacency in them. Now she watched the increasing strain on her sister's face, the tight whiteness of her nose, as if the ample homeliness of the meal in the barny breezes of the large old vicarage were a final offense to her taste.

"Oh, really?" or "Yes, charming," were all she seemed to be able to say to anyone about anything.

"Poor Sarah," Ann said, genuine in her sympathy, "this isn't your idea of a party."

"Charming," Sarah said.

Ann thought to ask about her nephews, who were busy about the war, outranking everyone else's children. The competitive habit of mind was so far lost to Ann that she couldn't think what to reply.

"We were surprised when Tim went off with the Canadians," Sarah said.

"Were you? I wasn't."

"Well, he's a bit of a rebel, I guess, and that's natural."

Ann thought of Timmy and the eggs, but in wanting to tell that story, her good humor wavered.

"Are you ever going to come home and visit us?" Sarah asked.

"It's hard to get away, with cows and chickens to think about, and we don't have a car anymore, just the truck and the tractor."

"No car?"

"No," Ann said. "We don't really need one. The truck gets us to church and into Hanover when we need to go."

She felt a faint defiance. Why? What difference did it make? But she needed to withdraw into the friendships around her. The next time she approached Sarah, it was at the party's end, people already leaving. Sarah was talking to Fran in the hallway.

" . . . a home of your own?"

"I have a home of my own," Fran answered.

"But, my dear, with an old woman! And there must be the gossip to contend with, if nothing else."

"Gossip?" Ann interrupted.

Sarah did not answer.

"We must go," her husband was saying now. "Ann, if there's a champagne bill . . . anything like that, just call me."

Ann smashed bottles rather than eggs, hurling them onto the terrace so happily and foolishly built that first summer, until it was a sea of broken glass she would have walked into had not her elected minister wrestled her into the house and fought like the angel with her until she was still. Joyce had taken Timmy to a friend's. Fran sat in front of the fire, drinking tea.

"I think she'll sleep it off now," the minister said. "If she starts again in the morning, call me."

Fran nodded.

"Fran, don't give her up just when she's winning, will you?"

"You once said there are things she has to do for herself."

"Yes."

"No one should be able to make her hate the way she hates . . . everything, even what's good in her life."

"That isn't the truth, Fran. Drink has a voice of its own."

"Gossip," Fran said.

"There isn't any gossip, and she knows it. The biggest scandal about Ann Bacon is that she sings Presbyterian hymns to her cows."

"And about me?"

"That a little slip of a woman carries hundred-pound sacks of chicken feed up to the loft when she has a perfectly good, good-for-nothing, alien spy to do it for her."

"I'd better clean up the terrace," Fran said.

The minister's wife was about to acquire an alien spy for the vicarage, a European cousin who was an artist and could not find a job until his English had improved. Though they had already nearly filled the vicarage with a large family of their own untidy, bright children, there was always room for just one more. To keep himself cheerful and to help pay for his board, he suggested that he give the people in the town painting lessons. No farmer was going to pay to have either wife or child taught such time-wasting nonsense, but the minister's wife did try to persuade the few people who might understand the need her cousin had.

"I'd never thought of it," Ann said, "but I suppose we all could."

"All?" Fran asked.

"Why not?"

So Timmy and Joyce and Fran and Ann all took themselves off to the vicarage, where they found their classmates were the other schoolteacher, a boy so quarter-witted he couldn't go to school, the minister's wife, and two of her sulking children.

Ann, confronted with a piece of board, cast aside her self-consciousness and with heroic goodwill began to paint.

"Mrs. Bacon," her teacher said, observing her first half-hour's work, "Is not a barn. Not to paint a picture so," and he gave the painterly gestures Ann had mastered for just such purposes as painting walls. She was indignant, but Fran gave her a warning look.

"I see," she said. "So how should I do it?"

With her skill and her curiosity, Ann soon found she was absorbed in painting not only during the weekly classes but all day long. When she was not actually taking an hour away from her chores to paint, her eyes were teaching her qualities of light as blessed to her as the air she breathed. "Look at this," and "See that," she was always exhorting the others, who looked with pleasure but without the wonder that filled Ann. So she must not only show it to them but paint it for them so that they could see what she saw: her trees, her fields, her buildings, the faces of the people she loved in God's own sweet light.

"Grandma Moses of The Fork," Joyce said, admiring a portrait of Timmy, hugging her mother-in-law.

Then Tim was killed, shot out of a foreign sky like a bird. For weeks Ann would allow no space for her own grief. She understood Joyce's too well. She was not even aware that Fran and the minister watched over her carefully, waiting for the inevitable suicidal rebellion. It did not come.

One morning when Fran and Timmy had gone to school and Joyce to the doctor's office, the minister stopped in for coffee as he often did these days. He found Ann painting a dark, winter wood. It was the middle of summer.

"I won't interrupt," he said. "I'll come back another time."

"No," she said. "I haven't much interest in it these days, but it's something to do."

"I've just come from John Gange. His oldest son . . . "

"I can't feel proud," Ann said, after some silence. "Their names on a plaque. Why aren't the wars left to us to fight, the old ones with all their old angers who cause wars in the first place? Why is it always our children's lives and not our own that we sacrifice?"

"God so loved the world . . . " the minister began, but there was not much confidence in his voice.

"That He gave His son to the evil in it."

"For the good."

"A high price for redemption."

He did not answer. She poured them both another cup of coffee, strong from being reheated on the stove, and offered the thick cream from her own cows.

"My sister's boy, too, last week," Ann said then, and suddenly she put her face in her hands and wept, something she hadn't done sober since her own young husband died.

Her elected minister stood, one arm around her shoulders, the other holding her head to his ribs, tears in his own eyes that did not fall, stayed shining there between him and what he saw.

"Thank you," Ann said finally. "I must go to John."

The town for its size paid a heavy debt to war, nearly silently. There was a war memorial on the town square, the first names, sons of those who had died in the battle for independence. Each war since had simply extended the list.

Ann bought six more cows and started raising turkeys for Thanksgiving, which that year, in some houses, would welcome sons home. The war ended in August.

Joyce, now that the war was over, talked of taking Timmy back to the city, where she could get a well-paying job and he could go to a better school. Fran encouraged her, concerned that Timmy lived so much in a world of three women, one of whom he did not even escape at school, and concerned, too, for Joyce, who needed more and different companionship. Ann, at the thought of losing them, wanted to argue, but she understood Joyce's need to be independent. As for the child, one was given them to give them up.

Their Poles were going as well, to better opportunity in the south. The boys who were coming home were, many of them, no longer interested in the hard life of their small community. They were going back to school or on to college instead, and their decisions influenced the younger ones, who also grew restless and ambitious. Ann could find no one to help her with what was now a fully operating one-man farm. But she could not think of getting rid of her cows. She had just won the state prize for highest butterfat content. Nor did she really want to give up being the community's egg lady. Being busy kept her from being lonely, she claimed. But at night, after work that began with the first light or before it, she could never lie down with the chores all done, and her nerves jumped with an exhaustion that often kept her from sleeping. Fran was getting up with her in the morning, working beside her until it was time to go to school, coming home as soon as she could to help again, sitting up after Ann had gone to bed to get her classes prepared for the next day.

"Ann," the doctor said, "at sixty-five you simply can't go on working like three strong men. As for Fran, you'll bury her next year if you let her work the way she's working. She isn't strong in the first place."

They sold the chickens. They reduced the size of the garden. They gave the house at the end of the road to a widow and her twelve-year-old son with the understanding that he'd help with the chores. Still the work was very heavy, and somehow they didn't have time, as they had had in the old days, to drive out into the autumn color, to take a picnic down to the river, to enjoy evenings with friends. Even visits from Ann's daughters were anticipated with dread, the house full of demanding guests when there were the never-ending chores to do.

"Why not sell the cows, Mother?"

If she'd told the truth, she would rather have sold her children.

It was hard to know whether summer with the house full or winter with the young stock crashing through fences and roaming the public roads, with pipes freezing and heating systems breaking down, was the more difficult.

"Why did we ever come to this God-forsaken place?" Ann would demand.

Around them other people, aging without sons to carry on the hardest of the work, were giving up. Farms were being sold to people from the city, either for summer places or for retirement. Even a few young professional men from Hanover were looking this far out for places to raise their children. Ann grumbled as much with her old friend John Gange as he had grumbled over her own arrival.

"They'll be gone with the first snow," she would say.

He'd nod, but in his own, now cataract-threatened eyes, there was the fear of winter. If his own roof caved in, he could no longer climb to mend it, and who else could? Who was left? Still, like Ann, he refused to sell his cows.

Then one night Fran hesitated on the first stair and collapsed. Ann rushed to her, knelt by her on the floor, lifted her up and cradled her in her arms. "Fran! Darling girl. Beloved child." The old woman called these names to the worn, drained face of her younger but also aging companion of all these years.

"Heart," the doctor said, as they waited for the ambulance. "And if those cows aren't gone by the time she comes home, I'll send her home to somebody else who deserves her."

Ann sat, alone in her house for the first time, outraged with herself that she could have worn Fran's life like undefeatable working boots through all of God's seasons and too many of her own. The taste of shame and fear in her mouth soured into thirst, no one there to stop her, no one there to know or care. Still in her memory she could hear a very much younger, quiet voice say, "If you go, I'm not coming after you . . . ever." And Fran never had. Ann had had to find her own way home and often then had had to go in search of Fran as well. Ah, not all that often . . . a dozen times in as many years? Ann did not even think in terms of fifty-fifty chances any longer. She did not need Fran to keep her sober. And she didn't need her cows either. She needed only her own strength to offer up for whatever Fran needed now, whatever the simple land asked, whatever the Caws or Ganges might require tomorrow or the next day. That was the bargain, deep in debt and credit, of accounts kept only in the heart.

"Grow old along with me. The best is yet to be," Ann Bacon carved over her fireplace, her own hand steady for the fine work of it, and when she had finished that, she sold her cows, every one of them.

"I'm trading the truck and tractor in on a car," she told Fran at the hospital. "You're coming home in style."

When Fran was well enough, they'd take a trip, maybe even down to see Ann's sister, who was very old now, lonely with a husband dead, a son, only one son left. She did see Ann's daughters often. Ann was glad of that. Then when she and Fran came home, maybe they'd make some new friends among these outlanders. After all, they'd been outlanders once themselves.

Ann Bacon walked out onto her stone terrace, built for her by a son now dead, once ankle-deep in broken champagne bottles from her daughter's wedding, a white-haired old woman, ancient-faced, warm and defiant-eyed still, breathing God's own sweet air in His holy light, glad to think that she would also now have time to paint again.

Miss Wistan's Promise

PACKING IN EARLY summer humid heat the winter clothes, bed sheets, towels, books, papers, in a trunk that had been similarly packed nearly every year for the last five, Belle was automatically efficient. She had few enough belongings to have no need to review them. Nor did she want to hesitate for any kind of pain over gifts received. She did not even try to imagine where or when the trunk would be unpacked again. Time enough to know when she was called upon to do it. Until then, all the assurance she needed was that she could set up yet another place, perhaps even with pleasure. She was not yet twenty-five, and if she felt more final in this leave-taking than she had in others, she knew as well that she was less finished. She was not running away, however it might look to other people.

Belle had been saying good-bye for a week, first to the people she had worked with, then to neighbors and shopkeepers, finally last night to Berta. A very good evening: first dinner at their favorite restaurant, then long, nearly leisurely lovemaking here in this room where Belle had then slept alone and was now packing alone. They had not pretended that it wasn't the last night. On the contrary, they were generously careful to make it a good one. They would write to each other. They would probably, after a year or so, see each other again. Belle had not been shy to say, as the last thing to say, "I love you." It was true, and she offered it that simply.

Anticipating this last day, Belle had not expected to be happy. She had hoped, nevertheless, to feel no unendurable pain. Trusted that she wouldn't because, perhaps for the first time in her life, she was making a decision in terms she could respect. She was going away not out of lack of alternatives, not out of fear or anger, but out of love she could serve only by going. She had not expected Berta to see the circumstance exactly as she did; Berta's understanding was all that was necessary. There was pain, but it was containable, and it wouldn't last. Once out of the place of their loving, Belle might even, in time, feel only wonder that she could, that she had loved like this.

The trunk was ready to close. The truck would be there in two hours to take it away. There was time now to go to give her keys to her landlady downstairs.

Miss Wistan expected Belle, iced tea set out for her as it had been on so many other afternoons, though usually for three rather than two. That extraordinary little old lady, a spinster who had spent her working life teaching little girls that intelligence is mannerly, provided Belle with as much lively conversation about contemporary architecture, music, literature, and theology as she had found in graduate school. As a landlady Miss Wistan had been as discreet as she was kind. Never in conversation had there been any reference to what Miss Wistan would have called "private life." For Miss Wistan it was just that. Nearly as certainly as Belle would not find Berta in anyone else, she would not find Miss Wistan in anyone else either.

After they had exchanged ordinary concerns, Belle settled to as honest a sense of the last time as she had the night before. It should be a good conversation, based on and developing from all the others they had had.

"Loving the best of any style rather than having a passion for nearly the whole range of one is at the same time too catholic and too rigid for me," Miss Wistan was saying.

Belle smiled in the pleasure of knowing that Miss Wistan had passions for Bach, T. S. Eliot, Gropius. Still, she was prepared to contradict.

"No," Miss Wistan stopped her. "Your standards are too high. In life as well as art."

"In life?"

"There are arrangements which people can make, not perfect, of course, but workable, if one cares enough."

Belle did not pretend to misunderstand, but she was startled.

"There are houses with two apartments."

"No," Belle said.

"Insisting on the best in this case leaves you with nothing at all."

"Only in one sense," Belle answered. "To leave before the tension gets too bad, before the tearing apart begins, before what has been lovely gets destroyed, everything good is saved . . . preserved."

"For you."

"For us," Belle said.

"She needs you more than you know, perhaps more than she knows."

"She can't leave him."

"Why should you insist?"

Belle looked at the prim-faced old lady and said, "I don't. I'm going away."

"It's a mistake, a very bad mistake. She'll follow you, though," Miss Wistan said with new cheerfulness. "If that's the only choice she has."

Belle shook her head. "She's never considered it."

"She hasn't had to until now."

"You misread her if you think she's been . . . complacent."

"Complacent? Oh no, not at all. In love."

Belle was tempted to take issue with the phrase but only to assert a private distinction. She knew herself to love rather than be in love with Berta, which meant for her that Berta in the whole design of her life took precedence over Berta as lover. If those two had not been in conflict, Belle had no doubt that she would have laid her life in Berta's arms as a nearly casual gift. But they were in conflict; therefore Belle's life became a threat rather than a gift. To be in love was to ignore all threat, to make every impossible promise. To love was to accept whole design, even in this extreme.

"I love her," Belle said. "That's why I'm going."

"If only you could be as old as I am in this one thing," Miss Wistan said. "Love is compromise, not sacrifice."

"Neither of us is any good at compromise," Belle said. "We've, after all, been trying it for over a year."

"No time at all," Miss Wistan said. "To form addictions, perhaps, but not habits."

"You're a remarkable person."

"But in this case not remarked," Miss Wistan said, but she understood that she was being asked to say no more.

Belle went back to her own apartment and waited for the truck to come. "She'll follow you . . . " Belle knew that daydream for a daydream even more surely than she knew Berta would not follow her.

She had been in love before with such impossibilities, even with "love as compromise, not sacrifice." That had been the basis of her first experience, again with a married woman. But Belle had been sixteen, without even the knowledge of rights to assert. That husband had been indulgent, perhaps because Belle was so young. She was still living in the fantasy of being an only child, desired by the mother. To be sexually indulged at all was a miracle for which any compromise was small. She had been without jealousy. Even when the first child was born, Belle's fantasy could shift, could make her feel she had some part in the conception. All the emotional forces that gathered then to shut her out she hadn't anticipated and couldn't deal with, for she was ready for any compromise asked of her, except that she not love at all. When the husband, for pity, made love to her himself, she finally did understand that she was the sacrifice. "Compromise *is* sacrifice, Miss Wistan." For that other daydream, "She'll follow you . . . ," Belle knew from experience as well, this time at nineteen. She was the seducer, not the seduced, and she had fallen in love, she thought, with possibility. But husband and child are not the only realities. In this relationship, there were parents and the church. Knowing the uselessness of giving in, Belle fought instead with impossible promises to take the place of parents, to be the kingdom of light. Everything.

> She is all States, and all Princes, I,
> Nothing else is.

But was not, but could not be the whole design of life, left crying, "Follow me," then returned unable to accept what was over, finally had to go nearly mad with grief to get out of what she had learned, without being able to admit, to hate. It took four years.

With Berta, Belle had never intended to fall in love. Berta had both husband and world. They made friends at the edge of that, good friends who were patient with each other's separate needs and responsibilities, for six months. They respected, as Miss Wistan had respected until this afternoon, each other's private lives, though neither would have been surprised at the other's intuition, in fact, rather counted on such unspoken insights, as friends with other loyalties do. What broke through that reserve was, perhaps, what broke through

Miss Wistan's: Belle's sense one evening of Berta's terrible acceptance of her marriage and her world. Her husband had been away, without explanation, for two weeks. Each evening Berta had gone home in case he might be there.

"Have dinner with me tonight," Belle suggested.

"I shouldn't. He might . . . "

"You can't spend your life . . . " Belle began before she could check anger.

"I am spending it," Berta answered quietly, but her whole face trembled out of control.

They made love after that, whenever they could. But Berta always went home when he might be there, and Belle never protested. She could not. She had no promises left to make.

"I'm sorry," Berta said once.

"Don't. When I can't stand it, I'll go. Until then, don't be sorry."

"All right."

The doorbell rang. Two men carried the trunk out of the apartment and down the stairs.

> Sweetest love, I do not goe
> For weariness of thee
> Nor in hope the world can show
> A fitter love for me.

How did it end?

> But think that we
> Are but turned aside in sleep
> They who one another keep
> Alive, ne'r parted be.

To keep her alive, whole, in a whole world, Belle was leaving. She had never been in love with Berta. She had loved her without false promises, without compromise. If she never saw Berta again, she had no sacrifice to remember, no insanity of sorrow. If they did meet . . . Belle refused to imagine it. She would stay free to live in whatever world there was. If Miss Wistan, in her passionate old age, wanted to daydream, let her.

A month later Belle looked back on that poetic leave-taking with incredulity. Why hadn't she known how angry she'd be, not only how bereft but how betrayed she would feel when she had to face her separation from Berta? Their relationship was no different from the other two. It was simply a more civilized way of failing. How could any relationship with a woman ever do anything but fail, given that everything and everyone else had higher priority? Berta was worse than either of the others, honoring a vow to a man who wasn't ever there against the real love she had for Belle. Only a masochistic moron would go on doing this to herself. And this time Belle hadn't even argued about it, had quietly folded her tent and crept away at the first sign she might be disturbing Berta's life. There was nothing to respect in Berta's kind of loyalty, yet in some part of her Belle did respect it. Why?

Half-a-dozen times Belle started letters to Berta which could have wrecked the illusion of understanding they had created. Sometimes because she couldn't bear the fact that it wasn't true, sometimes because her pride would not allow it, she destroyed those letters. She wrote instead about her new job, the city she was living in, the friends she was making, as if what she had done and was doing made sense.

"I've decided," Belle wrote, "to find out something about social life."

Two weeks after she met Timothy, she wrote again to Berta and said, "I'm happy."

Berta answered, "I'm happy for you."

Belle decided to live with Timothy, who was bisexual enough himself, he said, to have no trouble with the fact that she had been attracted to women. He was a good-looking, cheerful man with an easy self-confidence.

"I wouldn't ever want to live with a man, of course," he said.

"Don't be so sure," Belle said. "I said that, too, until several months ago."

What surprised Belle more than its being pleasant enough in bed was the extraordinary social ease of being with Timothy in public. She did not have to be rigidly self-protective with other men; she did not have to prove herself to other women. She was inside a solidarity she had not known existed. It seemed to Belle a remarkable bonus in a doubtful experiment.

"It's like crossing a border without any customs or immigration," she wrote to Berta.

"It's the country we're all expected to live in," Berta answered.

One night as they were getting ready to go out to dinner, Timothy said, "I don't like that dress. Don't wear it."

Belle was surprised but perfectly willing to please him.

A week later, at their own dinner table, he said, "Belle's not much of a cook."

When she confronted him with the unkindness that was, he said, "Remember, what you do reflects on me."

"And not the reverse?"

"Of course. You'd have every right to complain if I was late with the rent."

"I pay half of it."

"So?"

"Maybe you should have cooked half the dinner."

"All you had to do was ask me."

"You have the domestic morality of a good child, not an adult."

"I have the domestic morality of a man."

"It comes to the same thing."

He did not come home for dinner the next night. His explanation, after the fact, was a kindly, "A little distance clears the air."

"Not if you're not the one taking it," Belle said.

The next night he didn't come home at all. Belle didn't phone anyone to find out where he was or to complain. She was discovering just how much his behavior did reflect on her. She did not want to be shamed.

Timothy, uncrossed, was a gentleman. Timothy, criticized in the slightest way, vanished. Always cheerful when he came back, he clearly expected cheerfulness in return. It seemed to Belle a grossly unfair and effective tactic. She gave in to it, but she resented it. Every time now he corrected or criticized, she tried to think of a response that would daunt him as much, but she hadn't a manipulative imagination, and anyway it seemed silly. Instead, she tried to anticipate his disapproval and remove the cause, whether it was how she combed her hair or how long it took her to answer the telephone, but every week, then every two or three days, there was something.

"Don't be so petty!" she wanted to shout.

At least with women, the fighting had been over real issues, loving and the impossibility of loving. She hadn't fought with Berta at all. There were no letters now being exchanged between them either.

Oh, Timothy was often generous, and they had a good time with his friends, but Belle began to mistrust her acceptance among them. Every time a couple split up, it was the man who returned with a new woman, not the woman with a new man. Where was the country of the discards, Belle wondered. The idea frightened her, women alone together not because they wanted to be but because there was nowhere else to go.

She and Timothy stopped having sex, as Timothy called it. "I'm in a steam bath phase," he said.

"There aren't steam baths for women," Belle said.

"Pity," Timothy said in exact imitation of the Red Rose Tea ad.

Why did she stay on? Surely Timothy didn't any longer want her, avoided saying so only in courtesy, protecting what he referred to as her "more delicate feelings." Belle had no delicate feelings. She stayed on because she was both guilty and afraid. She did not love Timothy. If she had, she reasoned, she would have found it easy to please him. His irritation and now his indifference were really her fault because she could deal with neither in a generous spirit. But if she left him, she would have to go back to a way of living that no longer seemed a sane choice, at the volatile edge of other relationships as stupid and humiliating as this one.

Timothy came home with hepatitis.

"Oh God," he said. "This may be a dull way to live, but everything else is lethal. Don't tell anyone what I've got, please."

Belle was frightened for him and then, when he began to get better, sorry for him as well. He wouldn't see anyone until the telltale color of his skin had faded.

"Don't your friends know you go to the steam baths?"

"Are you kidding? Have you told them how many women you've taken to bed? We don't exactly advertise ourselves as the faggot and the dyke, a minor blessing but a real one."

"You're afraid of those people," Belle said. "That's why we're living together."

"Why do you suppose anybody lives with anybody?"

"I don't know," Belle said.

"You're not going to leave me," he said, giving an order.

Belle was too surprised to be irritated or frightened. However unattractively he was putting it, Timothy was admitting that he needed her. The revelation was not as startling to her as her reaction to it. She felt a stunned and stunning relief. He had quite inadvertently handed her back her self-respect.

"Berta?"

"Belle. Where are you?"

"In a phone booth outside a super market."

"Are you all right?"

"No, I haven't been since I left."

"But what's happened about Timothy? I thought . . . "

"And you were relieved."

"Oh, Belle, don't make me lie to you."

"I want you to tell me the truth. I want you to tell me that living with a man I don't love who doesn't love me is crazy."

There was a silence.

"Berta?"

"It is crazy," Berta said softly.

"I've been following your example. You're a lousy example."

"I agree."

"Miss Wistan said you'd come to get me."

Another silence.

"I nearly did . . . "

"But then I wrote about Timothy."

"No, it was after you wrote about Timothy."

"Oh."

"Are you going to leave him?"

"Yes."

"I am coming to get you."

"Right away?"

"I'm leaving in an hour."

Belle went back to Timothy's apartment. He was lying on the couch reading.

"Berta's coming," she said to him.

"When?"

"Tonight."

"Your answer to the steam bath?"

"I don't have an answer to the steam bath."

"Is she going to stay here?"

"No."

"Are you?"

"No."

"Dykes don't make great nurses."

She could have answered in kind, suggesting that faggots do. She could have advised him to try living with someone he loved who loved him, but she couldn't really imagine that. She simply turned away.

"I thought you said she wouldn't leave her husband. I thought you said . . ."

Belle shut the door and went to the basement to find the trunk she hadn't unpacked since she moved in here. Alone in the storeroom she answered him as well as she could. "Today she said, 'It is crazy,' And she said, 'I am coming to get you.' "

When Belle got back to the apartment, Timothy was gone. He was well enough to use that device of his anger which had worked so effectively for months but which was now empty of anything but his vanity. Since she was leaving him, she was glad he had it. Berta's husband, too, when he got home to an empty house, would leave again almost at once. What Berta had feared for so many years would finally be a relief to her, too, as she drove toward Belle, keeping Miss Wistan's promise.

Pictures

KATE AND SARAH did not know Mackie Benson. Kate in Los Angeles on business had had a drink in the same room with her six months ago but could not really remember what she looked like. "Sandy coloring? Plump? I'm not sure," Kate said, trying to recall. "An old friend—or a good friend—of Carol's." With a sad story of some sort—but Kate did not say that to Sarah, since Carol had just written to ask them if they'd give Mackie dinner and a bed for the night on her way north.

"No reason not to, I suppose," Sarah said, characteristically unenthusiastic about strangers in the house but resigned over the years to Kate's persistent hospitality, offered not only to relatives and friends, but to strangers like Mackie Benson.

"It shouldn't be all that much trouble," Kate said.

"A time limit anyway," Sarah said.

Their last guest, a friend of Kate's brother, had come for the weekend and stayed two weeks because his orders were delayed. He was a nice enough kid, but precisely a kid, used to being a child rather than a guest. Sarah did not know how to ignore him at the times when he should have had sense enough to get out of the way, talking at her in the kitchen while she tried to cook, sprawled on the floor in her study listening to records when she wanted to get on with her work, even chatting with her through the closed bathroom door. Kate was good at drawing him off, but she had work of her own to do and couldn't be with him every evening. He had to talk, nervous about going overseas, but it was a long two weeks, the longer because Sarah felt guilty about wishing his orders would come.

"I'm really inhuman," she said on one of the few nights Kate had been willing to leave him to his own devices as early as ten o'clock. "I can't see why the government can't hurry up and send that nice boy off to be shot at so that we can go to bed at a reasonable hour."

"No, you're not," Kate said. "It would be better for him, too. Waiting around is just giving him the jitters."

"And since it's too late for you to talk him into being a pacifist," Sarah said, yawning, "I guess I'll stop feeling quite so guilty."

Mackie Benson was on her way to a job in Seattle; therefore, barring car trouble or flu or a failure of courage, she would have no reason not to leave in the morning.

"I wish I could remember what she looked like," Kate said, "but since she'll make her own way to the door, I don't suppose it matters."

"It would be just our luck to ask a Jehovah's Witness in by mistake," Sarah said.

"Or the Revlon representative," Kate suggested.

"I'd rather lipstick than the *Watch Tower*."

Easy, unreal choices. Kate watched Sarah as she got up to start their dinner. It seemed to her remarkable that, in the ten years they had lived together, she had not become less obsessive in her need of people or Sarah more casually interested in them. The only change — and it had been a very gradual one — was that they had stopped arguing about people. The difference mattered less than it used to. Like the awkward counter that ran down the center of their kitchen, they'd learned, after a number of bruisings, to walk around it with skill and respect.

Mackie Benson — the kind of name that put Sarah off. And what was the sad story? Something to do with the service, was it? Or a particularly bad love affair? Both, probably. It didn't matter. She'd only be here for the night. Kate turned to the financial page and reached for a pencil. If she was honest about it, she liked their uninterrupted ritual as much as Sarah did. But so lucky and sweet a peace had to be shared occasionally, not so much out of an appetite for company — though sometimes it was as simple as that — as out of a sense of requirement; a loony, guilty notion about community that in practice more often illuminated the motives for murder than for love. Still, if there was enough food in the house, if there was an unused bed that someone needed or wanted, Kate still offered, "Why not?" to Sarah's "Why?" And Sarah had the grace not to answer.

They did not discuss Mackie Benson again until the day before she was to arrive, when Sarah asked, "Is Mackie Benson 'company'?" to which Kate replied firmly, "Yes, she is." That meant that Kate did the cooking. It was not a bargain to pacify Sarah. Simply, for all Sarah's reluctance about people, she was better with them than Kate for the first hour; so Sarah always coped with the initial shock of the invasion as if it were exactly what she wanted to do, while Kate observed briefly from behind a drink tray and then retreated to the kitchen. Later, in front of the fire, when small talk turned to silence or confession or urgent argument, Sarah refilled coffee cups or brought in drinks, lingering in the kitchen to tidy, and if the guests were spending the night, she quite often gradually disappeared altogether, not to be seen until breakfast the next morning, less innocent of the griefs of the night before than she could pretend, in order to reassure everyone that it was, indeed, a new day.

As it happened, Sarah and Kate arrived home from work at the moment Mackie Benson also found herself at the house. There was an awkward hurry of getting out of cars, Kate fumbling an introduction which Mackie and Sarah both talked through, all three coming to the ends of their sentences together. But Sarah collected them all into the possibility of going inside where there were ordinary and comfortable things to do.

"Plump!" Sarah said out of the side of her mouth after she had shown Mackie to the ground-floor guest room and was passing Kate in the hall on the way to the kitchen.

Kate shrugged, but she was puzzled. Surely she would have remembered that shape if she had seen it before, because it was extraordinary. From the back, which was their first view of Mackie as she got out of the car, she was fairly broad-shouldered, trim-hipped with slight but pleasant legs. When she turned around, she was like nothing so much as a primitive fertility symbol, all breast and belly. But her hair was sandy and soft, brows and lashes fading into her face, which was faintly familiar to Kate—an earnest face with that expression about the mouth of people who have had their teeth straightened. Odd. Kate paused in front of the open refrigerator door to try to think what she was supposed to be doing.

"Can I help?" Mackie asked from the doorway.

"Oh, no thanks. I'll be in with drinks in a minute. What do you like?"

"I've brought some gin," Mackie said, offering a paper bag which had in it not only a bottle of gin but a bottle of whisky as well.

Kate minded that at the same time that it pleased her. It was the sort of mistake she was apt to make herself when she was a guest, nervous to do more than was necessary. She knew in her own generosity the fear of being indebted, but she'd rather greet it in someone else than the mindless dependence she expected and felt required by.

Sarah and Mackie had settled to pleasantries about Carol, Southern California, freeway driving, topics about which Kate could never think of a thing to say unless she could ask questions more personal than were appropriate or introduce political issues into what were offered as weather reports. But she sat down with her drink for the ten minutes she considered polite, watching Sarah with the mixture of wonder and relief she always had at Sarah's ease and kindness. Just before Kate was about to get up to check things on the stove, Mackie stood up, went quickly to the front door and out of the house without a word of explanation.

"Did she leave her cigarettes in the car?" Sarah asked, surprised.

"I don't know."

They both sat for a moment, looking at each other. Then Kate got up and walked to the window. Mackie was standing on the front lawn, her back to the house. "What is it?" Sarah asked.

"She's just standing there."

"Did I say something?"

"I can't imagine that you did," Kate answered, watching Mackie. "You'd better turn on the back burner. I'll see what's the matter."

"She seemed perfectly all right, didn't she?" Sarah asked.

"Yes," Kate agreed, still watching. Then she turned away from the window and went to the front door.

Mackie did not turn around, though she must have heard Kate coming toward her. When Kate put a tentative hand on her arm, she flinched slightly.

"Is there anything wrong, Mackie?"

"No, no—nothing's wrong. It's just such a lovely evening . . . so cool," Mackie said, still turned away from Kate.

"Do you want to stay out here? There're chairs in the back."

"Oh, no thanks. I'll be in in a minute," Mackie answered, her voice ridiculously cheerful. "In just a minute."

Kate waited briefly, then turned and went back into the house

"What is it?" Sarah asked.

"I don't know. She said it was such a lovely evening. I asked her if she wanted to sit in the garden, but she said no, she'd be in in a minute."

"What's the matter with her?" Sarah asked, half concerned, half impatient.

"The vapors," Kate said. "I think she'll be all right, left alone for a minute. "Here, I'll do that now."

"What am I supposed to do?"

"Go back to the living room. Read the paper. When she comes in, offer her the funnies."

"Are you joking?" Sarah asked.

"No. I think she's just nervous or upset about something. Give her something to hide behind."

"I can't do that," Sarah said. "You read the paper."

"All right. I'm sorry, darling."

"It's hardly your fault," Sarah said. "If I want to be irritated, I'll be irritated with Carol."

Kate sat down in her chair and reached for the financial page. She was halfway down the mutual funds when the front door opened and closed and Mackie came back into the room.

"Funnies?" Kate asked. "Front page?"

"I always like the want ads," Mackie said, "in a different city."

Kate found them for her, and they read together until Kate got up to make another drink.

"Is Sarah cooking?" Mackie asked. "I thought you did."

"Well, we both do," Kate said. "It just depends . . . "

"That's nice," Mackie said, the paper firmly in front of her. "I don't like roles," and as Kate was leaving the room, she added, "but I would have thought until I saw you in the kitchen that Sarah did all the cooking."

"Is she reading the funnies?" Sarah asked.

"No, the want ads."

"I don't even know how to make this sauce," Sarah said.

"You don't need that much milk," Kate said. "Drink up and I'll give you a refill."

At the dinner table, Sarah asked Mackie about the job she was going to.

"I think it's going to be very good," Mackie said, still with a strained cheerfulness. "I've lived an awfully marginal life financially since I got out of the service—part-time jobs and that sort of thing. It wasn't easy to decide to move, but there isn't anything like this job for me in Los Angeles. Anyway, it was time for me to get out. You know what it's like: if you live alone, whether you've got friends or not, the phone never rings. In Seattle it's going to be different, a whole new life. I'm going to have money so that I can live in an apartment, maybe even a house. No more rented rooms. I'm going to love the job. And eventually I'm going to find somebody to live with, even if I have to bar cruise to do it. I hear the bars in Seattle aren't bad . . . "

Mackie looked from Kate to Sarah as if they might know.

"It sounds marvelous," Sarah said, her own voice slightly strained in politeness.

"Yes, well, I hope it will be," Mackie said, the energy going out of her voice.

"I'm sure it will," Kate said.

"I wonder if rents are higher," Mackie said. "What would your rent be for a place like this?"

"I don't really know," Kate said.

"You own this house?" Mackie asked. "Well, that's different, of course. I'd never be able to do that. All those years I didn't really make any money at all. And I'm bad with it. I do funny things with it—like, for instance, I save it around the house, not just quarters and things like that, but twenty-dollar bills; so I'm never really sure how much I've got. I just have to rummage around and hope it will add up to rent or whatever else I've got to pay. Still, I did buy a car, and if you knew how little I made, you'd be impressed with that. Maybe I'll be better about money when I have some. Do you suppose people change like that? I don't remember being so bad in the service, but I was really just a kid then, and they take care of nearly everything for you anyway . . . " and again the energy of voice failed.

"I think people do change," Sarah said.

"Having enough money makes a lot of difference," Kate said.

With that encouragement, Mackie started up again, faded out again, took strength from more encouragement, went on—or went round—for she said essentially the same things over and over again: the new job was going to be ideal; she'd find someone to live with; it was not good to live alone; she was bad about money.

"Living alone does things to you, and nobody wants to hear about that. You can't just call up a friend and say you're going crazy, can you? People say, 'Why don't you go out?' You can't explain that you've been alone so long you're afraid of people. That sounds like a contradiction, but it isn't. For instance, for a little while after I got here, I thought, 'It's just no good, Mackie. You can't stay here. You can't dump yourself on people you don't even know.' I'm over it by now, of course. I'm perfectly comfortable now. But when you're alone, you know you're an imposition. People are terrified of being alone. I think it's harder for people to go and see somebody alone than it is for them to see somebody in the hospital. You know, I got so I didn't go out for a week at a time. That's no good. Carol would phone and say there was this girl she wanted me to meet, but I couldn't just go over there and meet some girl. Some people can, but I'm not the kind of person who can just go to bed with somebody. I'm not attracted to that many people."

"Shall we have coffee in the living room?" Kate asked.

"I'll get it," Sarah said, quickly on her feet.

"Don't you want to do the dishes first?" Mackie suggested. "I'll do the dishes."

"We just stick them in the dishwasher," Kate said.

"A dishwasher."

"Let's have some brandy, too," Kate said, following Sarah into the kitchen.

"Isn't it awful?" Sarah whispered. "What are we going to do?"

"You're going to your study with work that has to be done. I'll cope," Kate said.

"Can you stand to?"

"Yes, love," Kate said, smiling at her, "I can stand to."

Kate took a moment's rest, however, staring down at the brandy tray. She knew that, in order to listen to hours more of this nearly unforgivably lonely woman, she'd have to get quietly drunk. Sarah would have protested, in the early years, "What's the point? What good does it do?" Kate didn't know. She resented the emotional blackmail as much as Sarah did, the self-pity and envy intended to make others feel guilty. But if you were asked to care, somehow you had to push down the resentment, to refuse the guilt, to understand the pain and be at least some temporary comfort. It usually didn't do any real good. As Sarah used to point out, it could do real harm. "It's just that I feel, there but for the grace of you go I," Kate thought to Sarah, and she also thought Sarah's answer, "Rubbish!" Kate picked up the tray and went into the living room, where Sarah was already pouring coffee.

"Carol's put on twenty pounds in the last six months," Mackie was saying. "It's all the beer she drinks. I've put on weight, too, but it's just that I don't bother to eat the right things. You don't when you live by yourself. In Seattle I'm going to take it off. I bet you didn't recognize me," she said, turning to Kate, who made a vague protesting gesture. "Carol says I'm too choosy about people. She's not choosy enough. I just couldn't do what she does, live with this one for a few months, then with that one, and even for those few months she's got to have weekend flings. She keeps talking about being realistic about sexual boredom; but when I love somebody, it seems to me that's too important to mess about with it. I don't understand how some people are so casual. I'm just not like that. I've had affairs, of course, but there's no point in that for me. It doesn't mean anything. You and Carol went to college together, didn't you?"

"Yes," Kate said.

"Was she like that then?"

"I don't really know," Kate said. "She always liked beer. Sarah darling, hadn't you better get to your desk?"

"I really must," Sarah said. "I've got work for tomorrow. Would you excuse me . . ."

"Look, neither one of you needs to sit around with me," Mackie said. "I'm perfectly used to entertaining myself. And I'm going to get off early in the morning; so you needn't worry about me. I'll just let myself out."

"I haven't got any work to do," Kate said. "Don't you want to keep me company for a brandy or two?"

"Well, for a little while," Mackie said. "But I should go to bed early."

"If I don't see you in the morning," Sarah said, offering her hand, "have a good trip and lots of luck with your job."

"She's a beautiful person," Mackie said after Sarah had left the room. "So quiet and kind. Just to look at her, you'd think she was as straight as they come, wouldn't you? I suppose I look straight, too. Men are always wanting to go to bed with me. That's the thing about living alone. They think they can just walk in and do you a favor. I hate that. I bet Sarah isn't all uptight about being queer either, is she?"

"I don't suppose she thinks about it much," Kate answered, forcing the coldness out of her voice, for though it was a vocabulary she hated and an attitude she found both embarrassing and degrading, there was a person in her living room who required her courtesy and attention.

"I didn't mean to be personal. I think you're both very lucky and very nice, that's all."

Sarah, in her study, could not hear what was being said in the living room, but she could follow the long rhythms of Mackie's voice, the occasional, brief, familiar tones of Kate's. Poor, darling Kate. She'd never, as long as she lived, give up suffering for other people's life stories. And people like Mackie could always spot the victim in Kate. She might as well have a sign around her neck that said, "I try harder." Mackie would go off untouched by or a little the worse for Kate's kindness, and Kate would carry Mackie's misery around for days without knowing it wasn't her own. In retrospect, two weeks with a restless boy seemed a holiday compared to this. Being yelled at through the bathroom door was one kind of invasion of privacy. Being inspected as an object of sexual curiosity was another, much, much worse. Sarah really did care whether or not that boy was shot at. She was not sure, given the opportunity, that she wouldn't take a shot at Mackie herself. Well, she wasn't generous-spirited. She did have work to do. And she had to get enough rest to be patient with Kate's hung-over despair in the morning. Also she'd have to remember to buy more brandy, because George and Ann were coming for dinner on Friday, and George was as fond of brandy as Kate was.

"I cracked up," Mackie was saying. "I got a medical discharge. I was really just a kid. I was eighteen when I went in, and I didn't know anything. I was always falling in love with other girls, but they were straight. The strongest word I knew was *crush*. What they did, they put everyone they suspected into one barracks, and then they planted a couple of people. It was six months before anything happened. I know it sounds unbelievable, but I was absolutely unaware that anything was going on. I suppose I didn't want to know. I never liked dykes anyway; they scared me. There were forty of us. All of a sudden we were all on barracks arrest and then we were interviewed, one by one. I went before the investigation without knowing anything. Four men questioned me for seven hours. I didn't know what they were talking about. One of them kept saying, 'You've been sixty-nining with your girl friend right in the barracks.' When I told him I didn't know what he meant, he drew me a picture. Then I began to cry . . ."

It was an old story for Mackie, told a number of times, lots of fixed phrases, but it was new to Kate, and she suffered the outrage of it newly.

"They didn't have any real evidence on me. There wasn't any. A lot of the kids were court-martialed. It took me a year to crack up. You see, I felt so guilty even though I hadn't done anything. It's such a lousy way to find out what you would really like to do. Most people—they meet someone they at least like. I got pictures drawn for me by a bunch of foul-minded, middle-aged men. Do you know how old I was before I did go to bed with someone? Twenty-four."

Kate poured them both more brandy. She could think of nothing to say, but Mackie had had enough to drink so that she no longer needed occasional encouragement.

"But that's over now. It's been over for a long time," Mackie said, a tough pride coming into her voice. "And the lousy relationships are over, too, the punishing kind you get involved with because you feel guilty, because you think you deserve abuse. For the last four years, I've been in love with a woman you wouldn't believe . . ."

Listening, Kate wished she didn't believe, but it was too familiar a story not to. Why were people persecuted into this kind of guilt, made ugly by it, cruel to each other? And who, relatively sane and relatively loving, would have either the patience or the need to do anything to help?

"I don't need that anymore," Mackie said. "This new job . . . I'm going to have an apartment or maybe even a house, and I'm going to find someone . . . "

Kate wanted to shout, "You don't just go out and find someone as if you were shopping for a car," but there was no point in shouting. Mackie was only trying to reassure herself, to sound to herself as if her life were, at last, going to be all right.

"I'm going to lose twenty pounds . . . "

Kate, drunk herself by now, looked at the heavy breasts, the round belly, and wanted to say, "You're lovely right now, the simple shape of desire," but she didn't. She sat very still and listened to Mackie re-tell the ugly past and then make hopeful swings into the future, only to come back to doubt.

"The trouble is, sex with most people just doesn't matter to me. I've only been really attracted to two or three people in my life. The rest is just role-playing. I lived with one kid who wanted to call me 'Dad.' I was never so embarrassed . . . "

Kate laughed. She couldn't help it, and Mackie laughed too. Her mouth, so earnest with straightened teeth, was very appealing in laughter.

"I can't imagine that," Kate said. "I can't imagine you . . . "

"But it's true. Isn't that awful?"

"It's hilarious," Kate said, the word slurring in her mouth.

"But I don't like dykes either . . . "

"I don't like words like that," Kate said, feeling very drunk.

"It's bar talk, I guess. I don't usually get drunk in somebody's living room."

"I don't mean that," Kate said. "I just don't like them."

"But you're not . . . you're lovely—to look at, I mean. Carol said she always had a thing about you in college, but you never seemed interested. When I saw you at her place, I thought why are people like you always already taken, and then I wondered if it was such a good idea to come here . . . "

"The world's full of lovely people," Kate said.

"No—not the world I know, not people like you. You don't even know."

"I know."

"Do you?"

It began as a clumsy embrace, but they were too drunk to hesitate, embarrassed. Then they were lying together on the couch in a long kissing, for Kate so sweet a relief that she wanted nothing but to go on and on kissing into opening desire, the longing of body for body there was finally an answer for, brief but absolute, against all ugly and grieving loneliness. But Mackie suddenly turned her face away.

"It's never any different, is it?" She said. "What if I were Sarah?"

"You'd be in bed asleep," Kate said, desire growing as heavy in her as grief.

"And sure enough that I don't matter to you so that she can sleep? This doesn't matter to you."

"It matters very much," Kate said.

"But not the way it matters to me."

"True," Kate said, and she sat up slowly.

"You're just a little bored, as Carol puts it."

"I'm sorry," Kate said.

"It's not your fault. I have no business being here. Single people are nothing but trouble. I started it. You didn't."

"Oh, shut up, love," Kate said, and she kissed Mackie on the cheek as she might have kissed a child. "Do shut up."

"You're drunk."

"Very," Kate said, leaning over Mackie now to rest her head on the back of the couch.

"It's not that I don't find you attractive."

"We're all attractive, love, every damned one of us."

"Not to me . . . " Mackie said, and she reached up to touch Kate's throat. "Sarah's very lucky."

Oh, lucky woman, beloved Sarah, how the hell do I get into situations like this? And how do I get out?

"You'd better fall asleep where you belong," Mackie said, suddenly businesslike. "I'm going to sit here for a while. I'll turn out the lights. No, don't say anything. Just go. I'm fine. Don't worry."

"Can I . . . " Kate began, trying to think of something to offer.

"Just go."

Kate went, not believing that she would be allowed to go so simply, but the drunken weariness left her as she climbed the stairs. She undressed in the dark, got into bed quietly, and lay still, wide awake, bitter, ashamed, bewildered.

"Darling?"

"Go back to sleep," Kate said.

"Was it awful?"

"What can you do?" Kate asked in the darkness. "What is there to do?"

"Has she gone to bed?"

"No. She's sitting down there. What am I doing here?"

"Do you want to go back down?"

"I don't know," Kate said.

"Go," Sarah said quietly. "Don't worry about it. I'm part Eskimo."

"She's so lonely," Kate said.

"And 'plump.' "

"Oh, Sarah!"

"You don't have to get mad. Go."

Kate got out of bed, put on a robe, and stepped out into the hall. The downstairs hall light had been turned out. She stood at the top of the stairs, furious with Sarah, furious with Mackie, furious with herself. Plump! Somebody Mackie had lived with had called her "Dad." Kate was suddenly fighting laughter. Sarah wouldn't even think it was funny. It wasn't. But Kate was trembling with laughter, there in the dark hall.

"Darling?" Sarah said quietly, standing at the door of the bedroom. "For heaven's sake, come to bed. You're too drunk to get back down the stairs."

"Somebody Mackie lived with . . . " Kate began, but she couldn't finish. She was laughing again.

"Shhh . . . " Sarah said. "Shhh . . . "

Sarah held Kate, letting her cry, irritated at her drunken silliness, troubled by the real sorrow somewhere in it, wondering why Kate never would learn that the Mackies of this world have to save themselves or stay lost; wondering, too, why Kate never could admit simple desire but had to have such elaborate and painful excuses. Maybe it was just as well. God knows how many people it would be if Kate didn't have to find excuses.

"You're so silly," she said softly, turning Kate to her. "You're going to have a terrible hangover."

"She reads want ads," Kate said.

"So do you . . . and want to answer every ad."

"Maybe somebody who can will. Maybe somebody relatively sane and relatively loving . . . "

"And relatively good-looking and relatively attractive . . . "

"And relatively free . . . "

"Which you really aren't," Sarah said, enclosing Kate, saying a moment later, "Quietly, darling, quietly."

In the morning, Sarah found a note addressed to them both which said simply, "Thanks and you're welcome. Love, Dad." Why "Dad"? Why "you're welcome"? Sarcastic? Maybe not. It was hard for Sarah to agree that she had anything to thank Mackie for; but now that she had left, perhaps Sarah could try. A tumbler of orange juice for Kate was at the moment more important. That was all she could really do, love and tend the fragments of other people that lodged in Kate.

"She's gone?" Kate asked, dressed and ready for work, remarkably clear-eyed for the circumstances.

"Yes," Sarah answered, handing her the note. "Why 'Dad'?"

"A sort of joke," Kate said.

"Why 'you're welcome'? Is she being sarcastic?"

"Not exactly," Kate said. "She resisted the temptation to draw us a picture anyway."

"Picture?"

Kate checked the temptation to furnish the picture herself, humiliation imposed on humiliation until Mackie had become an artist as fine as her tormentors to show Kate, for instance, how smugly unloving she was, how exploiting of loneliness, drunkenly groping at those lovely, large breasts . . .

"Kate?"

Kate shrugged and took her orange juice. Sarah would not understand Kate's guilt any more than she would understand Mackie's before those picture-drawing officers. What a solid barrier that was between them. Kate leaned on the kitchen counter.

"Well, all right, don't draw me a picture," Sarah said.

"No, I won't," Kate agreed, and smiled.

The Killer Dyke and the Lady

IF YOU'RE A killer dyke into leather, into aggressive visibility, it takes a lot of consciousness-raising along with a basic social conscience to call one of those expensively pant-suited, family-jeweled, narrow-nosed women "sister," particularly when her voice is pitched as low as yours but has enough breathy melody to be perfectly acceptable any-where, or almost anywhere. I wonder, shaking Dr. Ellen Compton's hand, the answering grip as firm as my own but not as assertive, why her sort of confidence is always attractive, whether for raping or for taking gentler advantage of for the advantage she has over me, Fay McBride with no title but Mac. We are peers, however, about to ad-dress together this room full of well-meaning heterosexists who will have less trouble being tolerant of me than of her. She could pass if she wanted to, easily, never mind the voice and the long bones. I could not. Oh, I have my own confidence, even arrogance; but there's no way I could condescend to this crowd as she does, just by being here, an aristocrat with impeccable professional credentials. If that makes me mean, imagining only a cleft palate could house all those silver spoons in her mouth, it can make this crowd meaner. But, as my leather belt creaks around my increasing Archie Bunker belly, I wonder if she has any sympathy at all for me. The woman introdu-cing us to this conference of social workers spends longer on the short list of my accomplishments than on the long list of hers. I don't like the fact that we are the same age, and take only small comfort in knowing that she looks older than I do, the skin at her throat, along her fine jaw, loose with the flesh that has melted away — probably be-cause I find that attractive, too. I won't look any different at sixty, "applecheeked," "sunny." Only my guts age. Just as the silence falls for my beginning, her elegantly panted thigh touches my tight blue jeans, and finally there is something to do with all this mounting energy. I look out at the bland courtesy of a hundred faces, and as my deep voice hits them with honesties they'd like to endure, I put my hand, perfectly visible, over hers, which is warm and full of pliant bones and tame as a domestic creature. Sister.

"That felt good," I say, as we sit in the hotel bar having a drink before the banquet. She's changed for the evening's entertainment, still in pants but autumn leaves now cover her breasts, and through the filmy sleeves her arms are beautiful. There are new rings on her fingers. If I hadn't held her hand through most of the public afternoon, my good humor balancing her charm, her authority in service to my assertions, I would have wanted to make a remark about those rings or those leaves falling, killer dyke screwing the upper classes.

"Very good," she says, sipping, of course, a martini.

I'm drinking whiskey, neat, instead of the beer I want. Other people from the conference stop at the table. A man or two finds it necessary to lean a hand on my shoulder. She has her cigarette lighted for her, distinctions which, because they seem to amuse her, amuse me. You don't go to these conferences to be hostile. But I know, if one of them laid a hand on her, a look in his eye to suggest, "Lady, all you need . . . ," I'd let him know there's not much difference between his fraternity and my sorority. Still, she knows how to take care of herself. Those rings are her brass knuckles. She can put out an eye without raising a finger. I don't admire that kind of brutality, but, damn it, it does become her.

As we walk over among the others to the banquet hall, she takes my arm at the curb, smiles, and says, "My first pair of bifocals. The curb keeps coming up at me."

They separate us then, but she's at the head of a table where I can easily watch her attending to this second-class meal with her first-class manners, and I wonder why I doubted even for a moment her reception among these mild enemies of ours, these knee-jerk liberals. She's one of them; and because they're all as upwardly mobile as a bunch of new-suited skiers, she's enviable there on the high slopes, but not envied . . . admired. And I'm as bad as the rest of them. I want to take those rings off her fingers, those expensive bifocals away from those ancestrally intelligent eyes, and expose those subtly braless breasts, and . . . and what? Eat the flesh? Sweet Jesus, meek and mild, let's put her through the eye of a needle.

"If someone's *disturbed* about her sexual orientation, don't you think . . . ?"

"Along with the American Association of Psychiatrists . . . ?" I interrupt the nervous heterosexist sister on my right. "No, all she needs is a good lay, with me or you. But that's not therapy enough to change her politics any more than it would yours . . . "

"I'm not really sure I understand sexual politics, and of course politics of any sort in a . . . "

"It takes a long time for a woman not to let herself be oppressed, in bed or out of it."

"But if she becomes simply an oppressor instead . . . . I don't like the language any better from a woman than I do from a man."

"A poem would suit you better:

> 'That ye resist not
> evil' falling
> limp into the arms
> of the oppressor
> he is not undone
> by the burden
> of your righteousness
> he has touched you.*

"I agree with that," the man on my right says heartily. "It was no answer to Hitler; and until oppressed people, whether they're Jews or women or homosexuals or Indians, I don't care what, stop cooperating in their oppression . . . "

That's the right rhetoric, brother, but there's one obvious difficulty with it coming out of your mouth. You happen to be the oppressor. You don't confuse or anger me, however. It is my sister there, across the room, against whom all my desire and all my revenge sing. Jacob and his angel were the same sex, too. I have done my social duty today. Sweet lady, enemy of the people, lift that fine, aging face of yours and see me here, wanting to eat your flesh. You're the only real meal in the room, and you know it.

Finally I am next to her again. "Let's get out of here," I say. "I've undone most of the good work of the afternoon."

---

* Poem by Phyllis Webb

Her eyebrows lift above her glasses in question.

"Let's do the bars," I suggest.

"A brandy back at the hotel, maybe," she says. "That's about all I'm good for."

She doesn't take my arm this time; so I put a hand under her elbow and help her across the street, but if I did not want her, I would not be so sure she is moving away. The caste of politeness is bone-deep.

"You don't go to the bars," I say, this time having my beer.

"No," she says.

"Just not your taste, or aren't you allowed?"

"Allowed?"

"By whoever . . . "

"Don't you live with someone?" she asks.

"Would that make any difference to you?"

"In what way?"

I have to laugh. We are both good at asking questions, neither of us about to answer any. Around us, the social workers are drinking and parrying, too, reluctant as she is to go off to more blatant climates. Having the two of us around, whether they call us "resource persons" or not, is as much of mixing with their "clients" as they can risk.

"Don't you think all of them would be more comfortable? Don't you think we'd be more comfortable somewhere else?" I ask.

"I'm still on Toronto time, and the only place I'm going to be comfortable tonight is in bed, but don't let me keep you . . . " she says, all graciousness.

"You're not keeping me. This is my town, after all. I thought you might like to see the sights, that's all."

"That was a great afternoon, Mac," a familiar, drunken voice says just behind my right ear. "They knew it would be, and that's why you came before the discussion about battered wives; you'd have seemed too good a solution."

She's by now leaning on my shoulder and leering at Dr. Ellen Compton.

"Betty Hall, Dr. Compton."

"*Formal*," Betty says, straightening to manage a stupid curtsey. "And *you* probably don't beat your wife, Dr. Compton, but I'm not sure Mac wouldn't. You can't convince me that belt's just for holding up your jeans."

"Betty's here as a resource person for the discussion on battered wives," I explain. "She's going to demonstrate the sort of woman who asks for it."

"Ver-y funn-y," Betty says, threatening to slump into the extra empty chair at our table. "Actually, Dr. Compton, though Mac looks like the toughest bull dyke in the block, she's really just a marshmallow; aren't you, Mac?"

"Just a marshmallow," I agree, knowing the only hope of getting rid of her is to be agreeable. She's at that stage of the night when only an argument will hold her attention.

"But, seriously," Betty says, "violence is a matter of class, not sex, don't you think? The only reason my husband doesn't beat the shit out of me is that he doesn't think it's 'nice,' and if Mac wanted to beat the shit out of me, she would; but everybody here, including Mac, is so nervous about being racist, sexist, classist, nobody's going to admit how anything really works. It was cute of you to rub thighs with Mac this afternoon, Dr. Compton, and that holding-hand bit was really sweet, but you wouldn't go to bed with Mac, would you? Or even to a gay bar, I bet. You don't need your consciousness lowered. Even being here is a bit of slumming for you, isn't it? And maybe Mac doesn't like the taste of your licked boots in her mouth either, but, as I've heard her say before, 'You don't go to these things to be hostile,' right, Mac?"

"And you can see how successful a teacher I am," I say to Dr. Ellen Compton. Betty's like having a drunken puppet on your knee, full of all the farts and belches you thought you could suppress.

"Why *are* you here?" the lady asks the puppet.

"To learn, to learn," Betty says, "and you've been very educational, thanks . . . " She's smiling at the next table. There must be someone there more interesting to harass.

Ellen Compton doesn't ask a question, even with her eyebrows.

"I've known her for twenty years," I try to explain anyway. "We went to school together . . . on the wrong side of the tracks."

"Would you beat her?" she asks, smiling.

"Would you?"

For just a moment, it's a game we're playing together and liking it.

Then she signals for the bill, and when the waiter brings it, she gives me a smile any dentist would be proud of and says, "May I?"

"If you're sure you won't have to hock your diamonds," I answer.

Because she is as quick with a retort as I am, I know she chooses to say nothing, which puts me at an unfair disadvantage.

"It would be polite to let think," I say, "unless you want to make me feel like a clod."

"I don't like double negatives," she says directly. "I have my sorts of protections, and you have yours."

"Quite right," I say, standing up as she does. "Do you go tomorrow?"

"Yes, in the morning. That's why I'd like to stay on Toronto time if I can manage it."

We go in opposite directions, I toward the street exit, she toward the lobby. As I turn out the door, I see she has stopped at a table to please its occupants with her good looks and good manners. Why would I want to take a woman like that to a gay bar? To flaunt her in front of my younger, more radical friends; to rattle her confidence in the minority she thinks she represents; to keep tasting the peculiar flavor of being with a woman of my own age. The oldest lesbian I know around here is ten years younger than I am. I realize, before I am half a block from the hotel, that I don't want to go to the bar myself, but I'm not ready to go home to my own company either. Will it look silly if I go back? I don't really care, as long as I find easy company for another beer or two. As I wait for the light to change to recross the street, I see her on the opposite side, waiting to come toward me.

"I wanted some air," she says simply.

I don't ask to join her. I simply turn around and take her arm. After we've walked several blocks in silence, she asks, "Am I not safe?"

"With me?"

"Alone," she says.

"Relatively, but you look . . . too expensive."

And wish I'd said something like "too vulnerable," which is all I mean. Again she chooses not to reply. I want to say to her, "Apparently tonight I don't want just a good lay; I want you." As we turn to walk back to the hotel, I dread being dismissed again, gently, politely, but I have no idea how to avoid it. I don't hesitate at the door; I go in with her and walk to the desk where she asks for her key. There is no point in telling her I owe her a drink. She doesn't want another, and neither do I. I stand with her waiting for the elevator, a dumb brute, refusing to look at her, refusing to give her the opportunity to say no. When she steps in, I follow. Is she allowing this because she feels challenged to make some kind of democratic gesture? I don't know. I am beyond rape fantasies myself. I remember her thigh against mine, her hand quiet in the cage of mine, her arms naked inside those transparent sleeves. I want to make love with her.

She is in my arms the moment the door has closed behind us. We kiss, slowly, curiously. I take off her glasses. She reaches for my belt.

"And now, ladies and gentlemen, exhibit A and exhibit B are going to show you what lesbians actually do in bed," she says, pulling my belt off. "First, however, they have to remove their armor. It comes in two styles," she explains, as she removes the rings from her fingers, "killer dyke and lady. But take a good look, ladies and gentlemen, because in a moment you may not be able to tell one from the other."

She is angry, very angry, but not at me, at them, and the undressing is not at all seductive; it's a hostile act against that day-long audience. Only when we are, in fact, naked, standing before each other like creatures ready for the gas chamber, does she say quietly, almost timidly, "You see?"

Her body is younger than her face. I shelter it with my own, appalled by her vulnerability.

"They don't matter," I say into her hair. "They don't matter at all."

"They matter very much. That's why we were there."

"That, sure," I say, "but not to hurt you."

I have a reputation for being a great talker in bed. I often don't realize I'm doing it because words are then as much acts as any other touching, sucking, entering. I can hear my voice against her rib cage, taste the tenderness of sound in my mouth. When we finally lie quiet, I can't think why I didn't know from the moment her thigh touched mine that this was how the day would end. She is already asleep, in Toronto time where she will be tomorrow.

Lilian

LIKE THE PAGES of a pop-up book, the scenes of love remain, three-dimensional, the furniture asking more attention than the flat doll who is more like wallpaper, a bedspread, a detail rather than the focus of memory. It might have been a way of dealing with pain but instead is the source of it, flat loss in so many really remembered rooms. Like a book, too, it can be shut and stored on a shelf with only the spine exposed, *Lilian*, without author or publishing house, but there is a prominent date, 1952. The twinge of pain is like the ache of a bone broken twenty-five years ago; you tend to think of the present weather rather than the old accident. Until someone asks, "How did it happen? Why does it still hurt?" A lover's question. Then there is the furniture again and the flat figure, and you, like a huge, old child, poke a finger as large as your old self once was into the flimsy trap of a very old beginning.

"There," you say, "are the twin beds pushed together. That's my desk at the foot of them. You can see the photographs I kept under the glass, the list of letters owing, a pair of gloves with the tips cut out of the fingers. It was very cold. That little gas fire didn't work very well, and it was expensive. We hadn't any money. That's the door to the kitchen, and that one went into the hall."

"But where is she?"

"Out, probably . . . no, she's in the kitchen. She's just come in from work and is putting on a kettle for tea."

"I want to see her."

There she is, simply a woman standing by a small gas stove, her back turned.

"Her face!" she insists.

But none of her faces is properly filled in. One has only the trace of a cheekbone, another simply a pair of glasses, and the hair's not real, put on carelessly by a crayon the wrong color. Her clothes, like those of a paper doll, are more important: a suede jacket, a gray skirt with two pleats down the front nearly to the ankles. She has a purple and gray scarf, a pale lavender twin set. She can be undressed. How long has it been since anyone wore that sort of bra? You'd forgotten about the peach-colored underwear. The body itself is an exaggeration of breasts and pubic hair, done in black and white.

"She looks very . . . English," she says, charmingly daunted.

You laugh, touch the very real red-gold hair, turn a face to you which you don't have to struggle to remember or forget, never sure which it is, and kiss a mouth which will never taste of tea. Her breasts are freely available to you under the pale green shirt. Trousers the same color are on an elastic waistband. You have made love with her often enough to know that she likes to come first, quickly, in disarray, one exposed breast at your mouth, your hand beneath trousers pulled down only low enough to reveal the mound of curly red-gold hair. To feel compromised excites her aggression. and you have learned not to be surprised at the swiftness of her retaliation, fake-coming to her assault so that you can both finally lie naked in a long feasting pleasure, where she can make no comparisons because her husband never does that, because you and Lilian had never even heard of it. When you came upon it in a novel written by a man, she was long since gone, but your need to taste her was as sharp as your simpler desire had been on those dark, English afternoons when she came in, her hair smelling of the tube, her face and hands cold, wanting a bath first to get warm, wanting her tea, before the ten minutes of touching which was all it ever occurred to either of you to do.

"Was she very good?" her voice asks, breath against your thigh.

Your tongue lies into her what is not a lie. The first woman is perfect, being a woman, even if everyone after that is far, far better, as has certainly been the case. Nearly without exception.

"Look at me."

You do. She is the age Lilian was, thirty. Nearly all of them have been, though you've grown twenty-five years older, will be forty-five in a few days' time. Her mouth from so much lovemaking is dark and swollen, her chin chafed, as if by winter weather. You are glad it is very cold outside, an excuse for her if she needs one.

"She's the only one you ever lived with?"

You nod.

"Why?"

"She was free."

She begins to cry, tears of a sort you had not seen until after Lilian. You wonder if that's one of the ways you've set Lilian apart, being able to remember that she never cried like that for herself or you. They are tears you have watched on a dozen faces since. You don't really want her to begin to talk about her children, but you don't stop her as you do if she mentions her husband, even to abuse him. You have not asked her to leave any of them. It is she, not you, who is unhappy about spending only a rare night in your bed. Most meetings have to be timed as if they were evenings at the PTA. She tries not to share her guilt about how she is neglecting her children's teachers. The guilt she feels about neglecting you is confused by the fact that you are never neglected in her thoughts. You are her private obsession. She leaves behind a toothbrush, a comb, a shirt to encourage the same state of mind in you.

"I must go. It's time to go," she is saying, wiping her eyes on the clothes she is gathering up.

You admire her fully realized body as she walks across the room. She pauses and turns to you.

"Why did she leave you?"

"Because I am not a man," you answer, as you have answered the same question a dozen times before.

"She married then?"

"No. Eventually she found a woman to live with."

She turns away again, puzzled. You would not have tried to explain further even if she'd stayed to ask. Once you did try. The anger that had obliterated Lilian's face and left her body grossly exposed in black and white, like a cheap polaroid picture, obliterated and stripped the questioner, who should have known then she was being raped and did not, flattered by the force of it.

The water is running in the shower now. She must go home, smelling as if she'd been to the PTA. On a better night, you would shower with her, mark her with quick pleasures. You might even joke about putting a little chalk dust in her hair. Tonight you put on a kimono, tidy your own clothes away, open the door to your study and turn the light on over your desk. You are sorting papers when she comes to the doorway, dressed and ready to leave.

"Are you angry with me?"

"Of course not."

You are never angry now. You go to her, kiss her throat, smile.

"God, she must regret it. Every time she reads about you . . . "

You shake your head, wearing your expression of tolerant indulgence for her admiration of your work, your success. The fantasy she is calling up is one you've tried to nourish for years but even the most outlandish fantasy needs some shred of evidence to feed on. You have none. Lilian always believed in your work. Success wouldn't increase or diminish that, and it would never bring her back.

"Don't shake your head. You're too modest . . . well, you are, about your work." But you have made her laugh now at the immodesties she enjoys. "You're so beautifully unlike a man."

Usually you help her to leave, but now you cannot because you so much want her to go.

"I want to be with you on your birthday. Why does it have to be on a Sunday night?"

"It isn't. It's on any night you can get away."

"You don't let yourself mind about anything, do you? I wish I could be like that. I'll be horrible to the children and to him all evening, knowing you're alone, wanting to be with you. Will you be alone?"

"Actually, I like to be alone on my birthday. It's my one antisocial day of the year. Well, that and New Year's Eve."

"Just the same, miss me a little."

You agree to. You know you will miss her . . . a little. Inflicting a little pain is necessary to her as a way of sharing it. When she can't, she won't come back; and you are slower now to encourage the break, though you know that to extend the strain on her for too long is a matter of diminishing returns. It's not that you'd have any difficulty replacing her. There is an understudy in the wings right now, who is free on your birthday, but you won't see her. She seems young, though she's thirty. Lilian at that age had none of the vestiges of childishness you notice increasingly now. She had not been raising children, of course, and was not absorbed, as all the others have been, with the ways of children and therefore inclined to tip into baby talk or take delight in small surprises. She had been as absorbed in her work as you were in yours.

"You're tired," she says.

"I'm getting old."

Again she laughs, as you intend her to, and now you must help her leave even though you want her to go. It takes only a gesture, a quick fingering into her still wet center.

"Oh, don't love, don't. I've got to go."

"Then go . . . quickly."

So beautifully unlike a man? So unbeautifully like one, and you've got so good at it that you manage this sort of thing very well by now. Then, as you turn back from seeing her out, there before you again, instead of your carefully tidied living room, is that pop-up book interior, the desk with its comic gloves at the foot of the shoved-together twin beds. You try to stay as large as the years have made you, as invulnerable to that anger and pain, suffered by a person twenty-five years ago, no bigger than your fucking finger, but your hand is on the desk chair. You pull it out and sit down. The gloves fit. The notes you are taking are for a book written so long ago you have almost forgotten it. The kitchen door opens, and there in it is Lilian, not a cardboard caricature, but Lilian herself. You keep on working. You do not want her to speak.

"Look at me," she says, and you do, surprised by the clarity of her face, afraid.

"You don't want a lover and a friend; you want a wife or a mistress."

"What's the difference?" you ask.

"You're not a man. You have to grow up to be a woman, caring as much about my work as I care about yours."

"I can't."

As she begins to change, fade, flattens to the cardboard figure you are now so familiar with, you grow into that huge, old child again, alone again as you have been at every beginning since, whether birthday, New Year's Eve, or love affair, closing the cover of the one book you will never write, *Lilian*.

In the Attic of the House

ALICE HADN'T JOINED women's liberation; she had only rented it the main floor of her house. It might turn out to be the alternative to burning it down, which she had threatened to do sober and had nearly accomplished when she was drunk. Since none of the four young women who moved in either drank or smoked, they might be able to save Alice from inadvertence. That was all. And the money helped. Alice had not imagined she would ever be sixty-five to have to worry about it. Now the years left were the fingers of one hand. She was going to turn out to be one of the ones too mean to die.

"I'm a lifer," she said at the beer parlor and laughed until her lungs came to a boil.

"Don't sound like it, Al. If the weed don't get you, the traffic will."

"Naw," Alice said. "Only danger on the road is the amateur drunks, who can't drive when they're sober either. I always get home."

The rules were simple: stay in your own lane, and don't honk your horn. Alice was so small she peered through rather than over her steering wheel and might more easily have been arrested as a runaway kid than a drunk. But she'd never caught hell from anyone but Harriet, rest her goddamned soul. Until these females moved in.

"Come have a cup of tea," one of them would say just as Alice was making a sedate attempt at the stairs.

There she'd have to sit in what had been her own kitchen for thirty years, a guest drinking Red Zinger or some other Koolade-colored wash they called tea, squinting at them through the steam: Bett, the giant postie; Trudy and Jill, who worked at the women's garage without a grease mark under their fingernails; Angel, who was unemployed; young, all of them, incredibly young, killing her with kindness. Sober, she could refuse them with, "I never learned to eat a whole beet with chopsticks," or "Brown rice sticks to my dentures," but once she was drunk and dignified, she was caught having to prove that point and failing as she'd always failed, except that now there was the new test of the stairs.

"Do you mind having to live in the attic of your own house?" Bett asked as she offered Alice a steadying hand.

"Mind? Living on top of it is a lot better than living in the middle of it ever was. I don't think I was meant for the ground floor," Alice confessed, her spinning head pressed against Bett's enormous bosom until they reached the top stair.

"You all right now? Can you manage?"

"Sleep like a baby. Always have."

Alice began to have infantile dreams about those breasts, though awake and sober she found them comically alarming rather than erotic, eye-level as she was with them. Alice liked Bett and was glad, though she didn't hold with women taking over everything, that Bett delivered the mail. Bett had not only yellow hair but yellow eyebrows, a sunny sort of face for carrying the burden of bills as well as the promise of love letters and surprise legacies. And everyone was able to see at a glance that this postie was a woman.

Angel was probably Bett's girl, though Alice couldn't tell for sure. Sometimes Alice imagined four-way orgies going on downstairs, but it could as easily be a karate lesson. It was obvious that none of them was interested in men.

"We don't hate men because we don't need them," said Trudy, the one who memorized slogans; who, once she could fix a car, couldn't imagine what other use men were ever put to.

Hating men, for this crew, would be like hating astronauts, too remote an exercise to be meaningful. Alice knew lots of men, was more comfortable with them than with women at the beer parlor or in the employees' lounge at Safeway, where she worked. As a group, she needed them far more than she needed women. Working among them and drinking among them had always been her self-esteem.

"Aren't you ashamed to sit home on a Saturday night?" Alice asked.

"We don't drink; the bars aren't our scene."

Alice certainly couldn't imagine them at her beer parlor, looking young enough to be jail bait and dressed so badly men who had taken the time to shave and change into good clothes couldn't help taking offense. Even Alice, with her close-cropped hair, put on a nice blouse over good slacks, even sometimes a skirt, and she didn't forget her lipstick.

"Do you buy all your clothes at the Sally Ann?" Alice asked, studying one remarkably holey and faded tank top Jill was wearing.

"Somebody gave me this one," Jill admitted irritably. "Why should you mind? You're the only one of any sex who has a haircut like that."

"Don't you like it?" Alice asked.

"It's sort of male chauvinist," Trudy put in, "as if you wanted to come on very heavy."

"I don't come on," Alice said. "I broke the switch."

At the beer parlor someone might have said, "Then I'll screw you in," or something else amiable, but this Trudy was full of sudden sympathy and instruction about coming to terms with your own body, as if she were about to invent sex, not for Alice, just for instance.

"Do you know how old I am?"

"We're not ageists here," Jill said.

"I'm old enough to be your grandmother."

"Not if you're still working at Safeway, you're not. My grandma's got the old-age pension."

"When I was young, we had some respect for old people."

"Everybody should respect everybody," Angel said.

"I have every respect for you," Alice said with dignity. "Even about sex."

"You know what you should do, Alice?" Angel asked. "It's not too late . . . is come out."

"Come out?" Alice demanded. "Of where? This is my house after all. You're just renting the main floor. Come out? To whom? Everyone I know is dead!"

Harriet, rest her goddamned soul. Alice mostly pretended that she never spoke Harriet's name. In fact, she almost always waited to do it until she had drunk that amount which would let her forget what she had said so that she could say it over and over again. "Killed herself in my bathtub. Is that any way to win an argument? Is it?"

"What argument?" Trudy would ask.

"This bathtub?" Jill tried to confirm.

"How?" Angel wanted to know.

Later, on her unsteady way upstairs, Alice would resent most Bett's asking, "Were you in love with Harriet?"

"In love?" Alice demanded. "Christ! I lived with her for thirty years."

Never in those thirty years had Alice ever spoken as openly to Harriet as she was expected to speak with these females. Never in the last twenty years had Alice and Harriet so much as touched, though they slept in the same bed. At first Alice had come home drunk and pleading. Then she came home drunk and mean, sometimes threatening rape, sometimes in a jeering moral rage.

"What have you got to be guilty about? You never so much as soil your hand. I'm the one that should be crawling off to church, for Christ's sake!"

Sometimes that kind of abuse would weaken Harriet's resolve and she would submit, whimpering like a child anticipating a beating, weeping like a lost soul when it was over.

Finally Alice simply came home drunk and slept in a drunken stupor. She learned from the beer parlor how many men did the same thing.

"Scruples," one man explained. "They've got scruples."

"Scruples, shit! On Friday night I go home with the dollars and say, 'You want this? You put out for it.' "

"So what are you doing down here? It's Friday, isn't it?"

"Yeh, well, we split . . . "

Harriet had her own money. She was a legal secretary. Alice remembered the first time she ever saw Harriet in the beer parlor wearing a prim gray suit, looking obviously out of place. Some cousin had brought her and left her for unrelated pleasures. After they'd talked a while, Alice suggested a walk along the beach. It was summer; there was still light in the sky.

Years later, Harriet would say, "You took advantage. I'd been jilted."

Sometimes, when Alice was very drunk, she could remember how appealing the young Harriet had been, how willingly she had been coaxed from kisses to petting of her shapely little breasts, protesting with no more than, "You're as bad as a boy, Al, you really are." "Do you like it?" "Well, I'm not supposed to say so, am I?" Alice also remembered the indrawn breath of surprise when she first laid her finger on that wet pulse, the moment of wonder and triumph before the first crying, "Oh, it must be terrible what we're doing! We're going to burn in hell!"

Harriet could frighten Alice then with her guilt and terror. Once Alice promised that they'd never again, as Harriet called it, "go all the way," if they could still kiss, touch. Guiltily, oh so guiltily, weeks later, when Alice thought Harriet had gone to sleep, very gently she pressed open Harriet's thighs and touched that forbidden center. Harriet sighed in sleeping pleasure. Three or four times a week for several years Alice waited for the breathing signal that meant Harriet was no longer officially aware of what was happening. Alice could mount her, suck at her breasts, stroke and enter her, bring her to wet coming, and hold her until she breathed in natural sleeping. Then Alice would go to the bathroom and masturbate to the simple fantasy of Harriet making love to her.

It wasn't Harriet who finally quit on it. It was Alice, shaking her and shouting, "You goddamned hypocrite! You think as long as you take pleasure and never give it, you'll escape. But you won't. You'll be in hell long before I will, you goddamned *woman!*"

"We're looking for role models," Angel said. "Anybody who lived with anybody for thirty years . . . "

"I don't know what you're talking about," Alice said soberly on her way to work, but late that night she was willing enough. "Thirty years is longer than reality, you know that? A lifetime guarantee on a watch is only twenty. Nothing should last longer than that. Harriet should have killed herself ten years earlier, rest her goddamned soul. I always told her she'd get to hell long before I did."

"What was Harriet like?" Bett asked on the way upstairs.

"Like? I don't know. I thought she was pretty. She never thought so."

"It must be lonely for you now."

"I've never had so much company in all my damned life."

To be alone in the attic was a luxury Alice could hardly believe. It had been her resigned expectation that Harriet, whose soul had obviously not been at rest, would move up the stairs with her. She had not. If she haunted the tenants as she had haunted Alice, they didn't say so. The first time Trudy and Jill took a bath together probably exorcised the ghost from that room, and Harriet obviously wouldn't have any more taste for the vegetarian fare in the dining room than Alice did. As for what probably went on in the various beds, one night of that could finally have sent Harriet to hell where she belonged.

Alice understood, as she never had before, why suicide was an unforgivable sin. Harriet was simply out of the range of forgiveness, as she hadn't been for all her other sins from hoarding garbage to having what she called a platonic relationship with that little tart of a switchboard operator in her office.

"If you knew anything about Plato . . . " Alice had bellowed, knowing only that.

Killing herself was the ultimate conversation stopper, the final saying, "No backs."

"The trouble with ghosts," Alice confided to Bett, "is that they're only good for replays. You can't break any new ground."

Bett leaned down and kissed Alice good night.

"Better watch out for me," Alice said, but only after Bett had gone downstairs. "I'm a holy terror."

That night Harriet came to her in a dream, not blood-filled as all the others had been but full of light. "I can still forgive you," she said.

"For what?" Alice cried, waking. "What did I ever do but love you, tell me that!"

That was the kind of talk she heard at the beer parlor from her male companions, all of whom had wives and girl friends who spent their time inventing sins and then forgiving them.

"My wife is so good at forgiving, she's even forgiven me for not being the Shah of Iran, how do you like that?"

"I like it. It has dignity. My old lady forgives my beard for growing in the middle of the night."

They had also all lived for years with threats of suicide.

"She's going to kill herself if I don't eat her apricot sponge, if I don't cut the lawn, if I don't kiss her mother's ass. I tell her it's okay with me as long as she figures out a cheap way of doing it."

Alice was never drunk enough or off her guard enough until she got home to say, "Harriet did. She killed herself in my bathtub." Nobody at the beer parlor or at work knew that Harriet was dead.

"I didn't ever tell them she was alive," she said to Bett. "So what's the point of saying she's dead?"

"Why do you drink with those people?" Bett asked. "They can't be your real friends."

"How can you say a thing like that?"

"They don't know who you are."

"Do you?" Alice demanded. "What has a woman bleeding to death in my bathtub got to do with who I am?"

Bett was pressing Alice's drunken head against her breast.

That night Alice fell asleep with a cigarette in her hand. When she woke, the rug was on fire. She let out a bellow of terror and began to try to stamp out the flames with her bare feet.

Jill was the first one to reach her, half drag, half carry her out of the room. Trudy and Bett went in with buckets of water while Angel phoned the fire department.

"Don't let the firemen in," Alice moaned, sitting on Harriet's old chair in their old living room. "They'll wreck the place."

The fire was out by the time the truck arrived. After the men had checked the room and praised presence of mind and quick action for saving the house, the fire chief said, "Just the same, one of these nights she's going to do it. This is the third time we know of."

Jill, with the intention of confronting Alice with that fact, was distracted with discovering that Alice's feet were badly burned.

The pain killers gave Alice hallucinations: the floor of her hospital room on fire, her nurse's hair on fire, the tent of blankets at the foot of her bed burning, and Harriet was shouting at her, "We're going to burn in hell."

"Please," Alice begged. "I'd rather have the pain."

In pain, she made too much noise, swore, demanded whiskey, threatened to set herself on fire again and be done with it, until she was held down and given another shot.

Her coworkers from Safeway sent her flowers, but no one she worked with came to see her. No one she drank with knew what had happened. From the house, only Bett came at the end of work, still dressed in her uniform.

"Get me out of here," Alice begged. "Can't you get me out of here?"

In the night, with fire crackling all around her, Alice knew she was in hell, and there was no escape, Bett with her sunny face and great breasts the cruelest hallucination of all.

Even on the day when Bett came to take her home, Alice was half-convinced Bett was only a devilish trick to deliver her to greater torment, but Alice also knew she was still half-crazy with drugs or pain. There the house still stood, and Bett carried her up the stairs into an attic so clean and fresh she hardly recognized it. Alice began to believe in delivery.

"This bell by your bed," Bett explained, "all you need to do is ring it, and Angel will come."

Alice laughed until her coughing stopped her.

"It's a sort of miracle you're alive," Trudy said when she and Jill came home from work and up to see her.

"I'm indestructible," Alice said, a great world-weariness in her voice.

"This place was a rat's nest," Jill complained. "You can't have thrown out a paper since we moved in—or an empty yogurt carton. Is that all you eat?"

"I eat out," Alice said, "for whatever business of yours it is. And nobody asked you to clean up after me."

"It scared us pretty badly," Trudy said. "We all came close to being killed."

"Sometimes you remind me a little of Harriet," Alice said with slow malice. "That's a friend of mine who killed herself."

"We know who Harriet is," Jill said. "Al, if we can't talk about this, we're all going to have to move out."

"Move out? What for?"

"Because we don't want to be burned to death in our sleep."

"You've got to promise us that you won't drink when you're smoking or smoke when you're drinking," Trudy said.

"This is my house. I'm the landlady. You're the tenants," Alice announced.

"We realize that. There's nothing we can do unless you'll be reasonable."

Bett came into the room with a dinner tray.

"Get out, all of you!" Alice shouted. "And take that muck with you!"

Jill and Trudy were twins in obedience. Bett didn't budge.

"I got you out because I promised we'd feed you."

"What you eat is swill!"

"Look, Angel even cooked you some hamburger."

"You can't make conditions for me in my own house."

"I know that; so do the others. Al, I don't want to leave. I don't want to leave you. I love you. I want you to do it for yourself."

"Don't say that to me unless I'm drunk. I can't handle it."

"Yes, you can. You don't have to drink."

"What in hell else am I supposed to do to pass the time?" Alice demanded.

"Read, watch t.v., make friends, make love."

"Don't taunt me!" Alice cried into the tray of food on her lap.

"I'm not taunting," Bett said. "I want to help."

Until Alice could walk well enough to get out of the house on her own, there was no question of drinking. She kept nothing in the house, having always used drink as an excuse to escape Harriet. There was nothing to steal from her tenants. She was too proud to ask even Bett to bring her a bottle. The few cigarettes she'd brought home with her from the hospital would have to be her comfort. She found herself opening a window every time she had one and emptying and washing the ashtray when she was through.

"You're turning me into a sneak!" she shouted at Bett.

"It all looks nice and tidy to me," Bett said. "Trudy says you're so male-identified that you can't take care of yourself. I'm going to tell her she's wrong."

Alice threw a clean ashtray at her, and she ducked and laughed.

"You're getting better, you really are."

Alice returned to the beer parlor before she returned to work. She wasn't walking well, but she was walking. She had been missed. When she told about stamping out the fire with her own bare feet, she was assured of more free beer than she could drink in an evening even when she was in practice. How good it tasted and how companionable these friends who never asked questions and therefore didn't analyze the answers, who made connection with yarns and jokes. Alice had hung onto a couple of the best hospital stories and told them before she was drunk enough to lose her way or the punch line. She only laughed enough to cough at other people's jokes, which, as the evening wore on, were less well told and not as funny. Drink did not anesthetize the pain in Alice's healing feet, and that made her critical. Getting a tit caught in a wringer wasn't funny; it hurt.

"And here's one for those tenants of yours, Al, hey? How can you stem the tide of women's liberation? Put your finger in the dyke!"

It was an ugly face shoved into her own. Alice suddenly realized why a man must be forgiven his beard growing in the night, forgiven over and over again, too, for not being the prince of a fellow you wished he were. Alice didn't forgive. She laughed until she was near to spitting blood, finished her beer and her cigarette, and went out to find her car. As on so many other nights, even a few minutes after she got home, she couldn't remember the drive, but she knew she'd done it quietly and well.

"Come on," Bett said. "Those feet hurt. I'm going to carry you up."

Drunk in the arms of the sunny Amazon, Alice said, "Do you know how to stem the tide of women's liberation? Do you?"

"Does anyone want to?" Bett asked, making her careful, slow way up the stairs.

"Sure. Lots of people. You put your finger . . . "

"In the dyke, yeah, I know."

"Don't you think that's funny?"

"No."

"I don't either," Alice agreed.

Bett carried Alice over to her bed, which had been turned down, probably by Angel.

"Now, I want you to hand over the rest of your cigarettes," Bett said. "I'll leave them for you in the hall."

"Take them," Alice said.

"All right," Bett agreed and reached into Alice's blouse where she kept a pack tucked into her bra when she didn't have a pocket.

Alice half bit, half kissed the hand, then pressed herself up against those marvelous breasts, a hand on each, and felt the nipples, under the thin cloth of Bett's shirt, harden. Bett had the cigarettes, but she did not move away. Instead, with her free hand, she unbuttoned her shirt and gave Alice her dream.

As in a dream, Alice's vision floated above the scene, and she saw her own close-cropped head, hardly bigger than a baby's, her aging, liver-spotted face, her denture-deformed mouth, sucking like an obscene incubus at a young magnificence of breast which belonged to Angel. Then she saw Bett's face, serene with pity. Alice pulled herself away and spat.

"You pity me! What do you know about it? What could you know? Harriet, rest her goddamned soul, lived in *mortal sin* with me. She *killed herself* for me. It's not to *pity!* Get out! Get out, all of you right now because I'm going to burn this house down when I damned well please."

"All right," Bett said.

"It's my hell. I earned it."

"All right," Bett said, her face as bright as a never-to-come morning.

Alice didn't begin to cry until Bett had left the room, tears as hot with pain and loss as fire, that burned and burned and burned.

First Love / Last Love

I SAID, "No."

It was very clear to me, not even at all difficult at that moment. I had loved Marilyn for such a long time, since she was hardly more than a child, thinking of her as I might have of a child of my own, with catching wonder I didn't have to express, not expecting to have to lose her as one does one's own child or lover.

"I am not a tree in your garden," Marilyn said.

It would have been unkind to remark how apt an image that was for me, watching her grow and flower. I did not expect her to notice and need me in any way but as a growing thing responds to space, rain, spring light.

Now I do see that she was not a tree. She is gone. I also see that I am not what I thought I was, simply part of the climate of her life.

I had forgotten what it is to suffer what she must be suffering now. It is not her pain that reminds me. It is my own. I am roused from sleep by erotic dreams of her, whom I have never held in my arms except to comfort.

"Don't treat me like an innocent," Marilyn said.

Only my dreams are obedient.

Awake, I see her everywhere, not only in a familiar gesture, angle of profile, but in the stupid, headless bust in a store, wearing the size and style of shirt she might have chosen. My womb, my breasts, the palms of my hands, ache so acutely I might think these were as much menopausal symptoms as sweating if I hadn't once, a long time ago, suffered so similarly for love of Justine, a woman twice my age. It didn't occur to me then that it was an experience we were sharing. Justine would never have admitted it any more than I would admit it now.

"I don't want anything," Marilyn said. "I mean, I don't expect anything from you . . . "

She does not mean that my body is nothing to be given; she means she wants nothing of my life, as if my body were as free of my life as of my clothes, could shed habits, needs, commitments, for erotic joy, and put everything back on again without difficulty.

"This is 1979," Marilyn said. "We don't need to hurt anyone."

I don't suppose I claimed the year as my ally when years ago I stood on Marilyn's side of the argument, as sure that we did not have to hurt anyone. I was thinking of other people, of course, not of myself or Justine, whom I desired and loved out of proportion to anything I have ever felt since . . . until now.

Then: Justine was a friend of my parents, well, really of my mother. My father liked her, but at those times when he was home, she disappeared into her own family life as wife of a lawyer, mother of large sons. The families did not mix, though perhaps we should have, my mother's daughters and Justine's sons. Justine didn't want it. She wanted instead an escape from the masculine world she lived in.

"How I wish I'd had a daughter," Justine said.

My younger sisters vied for that place in her life, feeling deprived with a mother so much less enthusiastic about their sex. Justine would help them fix their hair, cut out dresses, tease them about their boyfriends. Where Mother fretted, Justine indulged.

"But they're so pretty, so affectionate. You haven't got a football in the house," Justine said.

Though I was often claustrophobic with all the gadgetry that a houseful of women seems to require, I didn't envy Justine, who was able to convince anyone that male clutter was larger, more expensive, and worse. I thought, once I could choose my life, I didn't want the confusion of either sort of household.

"I'm going to live alone," I said.

That worried my mother, too. Everything did.

"But how lovely not to need anyone," Justine defended me, "to be independent, self-sufficient."

Justine seemed to me a very perceptive woman. I can't remember when I decided she was also attractive, perhaps after she had made some mildly disparaging remark about herself and I really looked at her. She was one of those freckled blondes who go tawny, and she dressed in dull golds, a camouflage? One of the colors of fire. Her eyes were golden, too. In affection or humor, she had a kind of growl for words like "darling" or "my love," which she called all of us.

"Aren't you going to the dance?" Justine asked.

"No," I said, "I think I'm probably a lesbian."

"Don't be a smart aleck," my mother said.

"Well, but I do think women are so much more attractive than men, don't you, my love?" Justine asked Mother or me or the troubled air between us.

Yes, I wanted to answer passionately, *or at least you are.* But there was no way I could suddenly blossom out of shy thorniness into a lover there before my mother's eyes—or Justine's for that matter. I had no idea how it was done.

Now I can wonder whether Justine was really in love with Mother, cast her net and caught me instead, a floundering innocent who hadn't known it wasn't air I'd been breathing until my lungs were seared with it, until my flesh burned.

I did run a fever. I lay in bed, whispering, "Fire, fire," and heard Mother tell Justine I was delirious. She came to my bedside, bathed my face, lifted my head to sip water, growling and encouraging, "My love," "Darling." My head resting on her breast, I fainted.

It was not an act, as so much adolescent love is portrayed. Far from exaggerating my feelings, I desperately tried first to recover and then to hide. Those horribly in love discover sarcasm. When Justine complained of growing old, I told her I was hag-ridden. When she said my eyes were the color of the sky, I told her hers were a smog alert. When she said I was clever with words, I fell silent. When she touched me, I shouted, "Don't paw!" And touched myself to remember her hands and had private names for her: "Athena," "lioness," "beloved," and saw her everywhere in everything sun-colored and hot, and was in torment, willing and unwilling to live. Near her I sulked; separated from her I pined.

"Really what you ought to do, you know, darling girl, is fall in love. It's time," she said.

"You're giving me your permission?"

"Of course."

"I am in love. I am in love with you."

In one of my recent dreams about Marilyn, she was embracing me, but it was Justine in her arms. Justine looked exactly as she had first looked, recognizing, at me, the fire flaming up in her unguarded eyes. If I had known enough to take her in my arms at that moment, we might, after all, have ruined our lives. All failed lovers rewrite the script, as if one sexual detail or another might have tipped the balance of pain into destiny, either tragic or miraculous.

Weeks later, she kissed me once. I still remember it with an intensity it doesn't deserve. Oh, why not? How many people can claim to have been kissed first by someone entirely desired as I desired Justine? It was long, gentle at first, then surprising, her mouth discovering so much I hadn't known I could feel. When she drew back, she looked at me.

"Is that what you really want?"

"Yes."

Ten minutes out of a life. Ten minutes more than I have had with Marilyn. Perhaps Justine hadn't ever been a girl in love with a woman and did not know how totally demanding that awakened appetite could be. She did protect herself.

"You know I love you," she said. "I know you love me; you don't have to prove it."

"I want to."

They sent me away to school, not only my parents but Justine, where absence did its mythologizing work. Justine was everyone from Madame Bovary to Lady Macbeth. I treated anyone who reminded me of her, from my English teacher to the president of my class, with grieving tenderness, as if they were dying of cancer. It didn't take much to remind me—a gold sweater, a turn of phrase, any line of breast. Sometimes alone I sat kissing the heel of my own hand and weeping.

I caught myself just yesterday in that forgotten gesture. It felt as regressive as rediscovering the sucking of my thumb. I am not only a grown woman, I am a growing-old woman. Could Justine have grieved as I grieve now?

"Why aren't there any happy love stories?" my mother once asked Justine, who heard the real question under the petulance.

"Because marriage is the end of them."

"The end?"

"Of the love story. It turns into something else then, an undertaking of children, mortgages, politics. Only lovers who can't marry go on being lovers, or anyway just lovers."

"Love is supposed to ruin your life," I said. "That's what it's for."

"Such cynicism," my mother complained. "People can love suitably and be happy."

I did not even attempt to catch Justine's eye at such moments. I did not know how to ask for what I wanted except by asking. I was easy to refuse, as easy as Marilyn has been, who honorably made no gesture while stating her case.

I have fallen happily, if not suitably according to my mother's lights, in love. What an entirely different experience it is! Only with the illicit is there an ethic of innocence, a high-mindedness that invites rejection. When I had a life in my hands to offer, I felt few other scruples, touched, teased, tempted, took as I pleased and still do. Did Justine? I suppose so. She certainly had no more intention than I do now of giving up anything of her life for what I assumed for her was nothing more than a minor amusement. Justine was my life, the whole of it.

Does love, to stay what we call *love*, have to be unequal or at least unbalanced? Or just impossible?

I eat and sleep badly. I am ill-tempered. And I can't talk about it. I, who have learned a combative frankness about sexual appetite, sexual freedom, cannot so much as mention Marilyn's name. She is not my life, no. It goes by a different name. Neither, however, is she casual to it. My life does depend on saying no, not because she is half my age, not because I am faithful, but because I love her and have always loved her, and I would rather lose her like this than keep her. She would wreck my life and her own. I don't understand why it is so hideously hard, something so simple.

Should I be guilty? Should Justine? I never blamed her for anything but a lack of sexual generosity, and compared with Justine I have been stingy with Marilyn.

I miss her, but not as I would someone away and coming back. I miss her as if she were dead. I am in intense, helpless mourning. It cannot go on as long as it did for Justine—years. This time I not only know what it is but also that I do not want it. I also know, when it is over, I will never feel this way again. What will be left to me are real deaths, and this is as it should be.

Oh, waking from one of these erotic dreams, I can try to escape my own clarity, rationalize a short holiday, a weekend, even a night — Justine did, after all, kiss and touch me, and I survived to live my kind of happily-ever-after. If I am incapable of killing Marilyn in my dreams, why am I so adamant about her banishment? I could not, otherwise, survive losing her. And I have to lose her to her own life, which cannot be lived at the edge of mine.

If she came through the door at this moment, dropped a kiss on the top of my head as she has for years, offered me a bite of sandwich or a candy bar, neither of us could pretend we were back at the other side of knowing. Even I wouldn't want to. This suffering, this last love like the first, is so unexpected, so searingly beautiful, who would call back Eden? Justine loved me like this. That is my consolation, to know after all these years that I also caused the exquisite pain I suffered. What is Marilyn's? Must she wait as long as I have waited, her mouth filling with foreign teeth, her sight failing, her thighs beginning to wither, for some young girl to betray my secret? At least as long, when there is nothing left to forgive, for only then will she be able to say, "No," in her turn.

Perhaps it is so hard because it is so simple, just that. Marilyn.

Sightseers in Death Valley

DRIVING INTO DEATH Valley at Christmas time—the time of year it was first discovered by white men—is something like arriving in a place only months after it has been bombed. The disaster here, of course, is simply summer with its hundred-and-twenty-degree heat, its infrequent but violent rains, its windstorms. Permanent signs along the main roads give directions for driving in the desert, for survival. Neither whiskey nor urine is a real substitute for water. Temporary signs indicate which roads are closed, buried in sand drifts, or washed out by flash floods. It is a fragile land, a weather bed reformed by any caprice of the wind, for very little grows here except desert holly and mesquite, and on the sand dunes even those disappear, as they do also in the salt flats where only the crystals themselves grow, pushing up through the silt surface in arthritic gestures. By now, though the signs of summer desecration are everywhere, the air is cool and still. The mountains, barren, exposing geological violence as remotely slow-moving as the wind is swift, are nearly gaudy under the winter sun, red, blue green, violet, yellow. The desert holly is in bloom with small outcroppings the color of blood. At the inn it has been tied with red ribbon and put on every door.

The population of the valley is at its largest this time of year, and its makeup is similar to those of other sunny Christmas resorts. Many Jewish families are trying to save their children from the disaster of Christmas itself. A number of young grandparents are still struggling to recover rather than swallow pride after the first rift with young in-laws. Childless couples with two incomes can afford a winter holiday. Single women in groups of three are too old to keep going home for Christmas, and an occasional couple, lesbian, perhaps can't. A few whole Christian families, including teen-aged children and grandparents, are affluent enough to celebrate Christmas away from home. The very old, escaping winter, need the sun and the hot springs more than great-grandparental joy.

Like most places, there is lots to do or nothing. Children can ride hard-mouthed, exhausted little horses that walk into and out of Breakfast Canyon once a day, bully a parent into going to the swimming pool, play volleyball, shuffleboard. There is an eighteen-hole golf course. There are two museums. In the evening there is dancing, a movie, a slide show, a naturalist's talk. For the campers any place that is warm and light for those first early hours of the winter night is a good place. The ranch saloon usually closes at nine-thirty instead of the advertised midnight because only employees are still drinking along with Sky King, a little man in a cowboy hat who flies charters into the Grand Canyon or sells tickets to the movie. No place is crowded. Nobody is rowdy. People who want real night life are in Las Vegas.

At the ranch swimming pool, there is a large sign which says, NO LIFEGUARD IS ON DUTY. The handsome man who is obviously paid to sit there reads a book or talks to the guests. If he missed a drowning, he'd only be obeying the sign. Miss Jensen, whose friend has taken to the horses, is reading T. S. Eliot. Mrs. Dirkheimer, whose five-year-old son has whined his father into a game of shuffleboard, stares at Miss Jensen.

"Do you just like T. S. Eliot?"

"Heavens no," Miss Jensen answers. "I teach him."

"My husband is interested in literature," Mrs. Dirkheimer says. "As a hobby."

"I breed bulldogs," Miss Jensen says, a lie which will allow her to go on reading.

Miss Jensen is not fond of animals, even human animals, but she has a large amount of passive tolerance. Later in the day she will find her friend, and they will collect rocks, which make the best companions.

Marne Ginter is saying to Alice Faymoor, "Christmas with kids just turns into gimme, gimme, gimme. So I said to Maureen, 'Don't worry about us. You and Joe and the kids go ahead and do your own thing. We're taking a vacation.' 'A vacation!' she says, 'at this time of year? People'll think we had a fight or something.' 'Well, so, is truth going to hurt them?' I said. 'But where are you going to go at

Christmas? 'Death Valley,' I said   Do you know, she started crying?"

Marne and Alice are laughing. The sun is hot. Today isn't Christmas.

"Listen, Hymen," his father says to the three-year-old retching into the trough, "if you go under the water and you breathe, you'll drown and die. How many times do I have to tell you? You'll drown and die."

"How?" Hymen asks.

"What do you mean, *how?*"

"The kid wants a demonstration," another father calls. It's Dirkheimer, back from five long minutes of shuffleboard. "I'd like to give him one with my kid."

"You irritating your father?" young Mrs. Dirkheimer demands.

"Naw, he's not. I'm only speaking in the interests of science."

"Did you thank your father for playing shuffleboard with you? Did you?"

Miss Jensen closes her book, folds up her sunglasses, and puts on her white terry-cloth robe.

"Aren't you going in today?" the non-lifeguard asks.

"I've been," Miss Jensen answers, smiling.

"Hymen! Holy God . . . "

Hymen is retching into the trough again. He'll be swimming or dead by tomorrow.

"That woman," Dirkheimer's wife is saying, "breeds bulldogs."

"You're kidding me."

"She said so herself."

They stare after Miss Jensen, who's forty if she's a day, never mind she's watched her figure.

"Well, you gotta have human pity," Dirkheimer says.

A nubile champion goes off the diving board while men watch in uncertain, parental lechery, except for the paid attendant, who is now reading *The Naked Ape.*

"For laughs," he explains when Marne Ginter asks, as she and Alice walk by to meet their golf-playing husbands for lunch.

"He's a good case for skin cancer," Alice says. "If you ask me."

"I never liked a conceited man. That's what I don't understand about Maureen. To marry a guy like that. He is like that, Joe is.

Just plain conceited."

Though Scotty's Castle is a good two-hour drive north from the oasis of the ranch and inn, Miss Jensen and her friend discover it is not an outing for escaping the others. On their way there, they sight Dirkheimer coming over a sand dune on his knees with his tongue hanging out for his wife to take a picture, their five-year-old standing at a puzzled distance.

"He must take Tums," the friend observes. "His tongue is white."

"Probably the food in the cafeteria doesn't agree with him," Miss Jensen suggests.

They have brought their own food and electric pans, which they keep hidden behind the stock of towels in the bathroom. There is no sign in the cabin forbidding cooking; but since there is no provision for it, they have decided to be careful rather than to inquire.

Farther along they catch sight of the Ginters and Faymoors, who are collecting desert holly in a rocky field beside the road. Miss Jensen's friend notes with pleasure Marne Ginter's orange blouse, Alice Faymoor's aquamarine, colors attractive against the nearly subtle mountains.

"People ought to dress not only for the weather but for the landscape."

"It's against the law to pick that holly."

"Well, we're not rangers," Miss Jensen's friend replies, holiday relief in her voice.

When they arrive at Scotty's Castle, the man who is not a lifeguard at the pool is already there with an older man the women have not seen before. His Mercedes suggests he is staying at the inn, which costs at least double what it does at the ranch, with no way to avoid the dining room for meals. Miss Jensen and her friend have booked there for Christmas dinner.

The younger man smiles at Miss Jensen.

"He's got to be quite a buddy of yours," her friend observes.

"He's one of us," Miss Jensen replies.

"Isn't he just!"

Shortly the Dirkheimers, Ginters, and Faymoors all arrive, and they begin the tour of this unlikely, not mysterious enough whim of a man of uncertain taste.

"No worse than Longleat," Miss Jensen's friend observes, a comparison so absurd Miss Jensen laughs.

"I'm not crazy about all this Indian and Mexican stuff, are you?" Marne is asking Alice.

"Most of it looks as if it ought to be in a church," Alice says. "A *Catholic* church." They both giggle.

Alice's husband lights a cigarette and is asked to put it out. He is perfectly pleasant about it, but after that he yawns a lot; and as they approach the much heralded music room, he begins to sigh. Ginter offers him a piece of gum, which he refuses.

"Hymen, you can't go up there, it's roped off," a familiar father's voice orders.

"I thought that kid was drowned yesterday," Dirkheimer says quietly to his wife, while increasing the pressure on his own obedient son's hand.

Though the music room is large for a private house, the tourists are too numerous for the seats. The two men give up their seats for Miss Jensen and her friend.

"Show," Marne says. "For some men that's all there is."

The organ is badly asthmatic. Miss Jensen and her friend suffer for Bach. Alice and Marne stifle laughter. Dirkheimer wonders if he ought to offer to try to fix it. He built an electric organ once from a kit. Hymen begins to cry.

"At least we're not all on the same bus," Miss Jensen observes as they walk into the parking lot.

"It would have saved gas," her friend answers.

The man with the Mercedes comes up to them and says, "If you're planning to have Christmas dinner at the inn, would you join us for drinks beforehand?"

"Oh, I . . . " Miss Jensen hesitates, looking to her friend.

"Why not?" her friend asks lightly.

"About six o'clock then?"

"Thank you," Miss Jensen says.

"Did you see that man in the Mercedes pick up our bulldog breeder back there in the parking lot?" Dirkheimer's wife asks him.

"He didn't pick her up," their five-year-old corrects. "He was just talking to her."

"Maybe he doesn't know her terrible secret," Dirkheimer speculates.
"What's that?" the child demands.
"That she breeds bulldogs."
"That's not a secret!" the child says in disgust and turns out of his
parents' silly and incomprehensible conversation.
"That car, that diamond ring, that good-looking lifeguard: he's got
to be h-o-m-o-s-e-x-u-a-l."
"Maybe it's a case of birds of a feather," Dirkheimer suggests.
"Not those women!" his wife protests, shocked.
Dirkheimer shrugs over his steering wheel.
Tomorrow he will agree with Hootstein, Hymen's father, to share
the cost of hiring Sky King to fly both families into the Grand Canyon on Christmas Day.
"Hymen will probably throw up the whole way," Dirkheimer's
wife protests.
"So I was supposed to say no?" Dirkheimer asks. "You want to
play gentile-for-a-day instead?"
There is an enormous and badly decorated Christmas tree in the
ranch cafeteria, where Miss Jensen and her friend decide to eat on
Christmas Eve since, after a week of cooking out of their cupboard,
what is left doesn't seem festive enough for the occasion. There are
presents under the tree, which distress the children with impatient
greed.
"There's nothing inside them, Hymen," his father explains.
"How do you know?" Hymen demands.
"I know. Take my word for it," his father answers.
"We always have meatloaf at home on Christmas Eve," Marne confides to Alice. "It's a sort of tradition. I wonder if Maureen's made it
anyway."
"If I know Joe," her husband says, "they'll be eating steak tonight
and tomorrow."
"Not on Christmas Day!" Marne protests.
"The guy eats like a truck driver," Ginter complains to the table at
large. "Your daughter gets married, and before long you've got to
spend a thousand bucks to be sure to get turkey on Christmas Day."
"Or goose," Alice suggests. "I think they're going to have both at
the inn."

"Goose!" Ginter says. "Where are we? Merry old England?"

The Faymoors' older son is with his rich in-laws, an every-other-year arrangement in which the Faymoors are not included. Their younger son is somewhere in Europe. They don't even know where to send his presents, which are wrapped up at home in his closet.

The staff is gathering by the Christmas tree, both men and.women with big red crepe-paper bows around their necks.

"They're going to sing Christmas carols," Hymen's mother warns, wanting to clap her hands over Hymen's ears.

"It's probably going on even in Jerusalem," Dirkheimer says, preaching resignation.

To their relief and Miss Jensen's disgust the first song is "Rudolph, the Red-Nosed Reindeer." When "I'm Dreaming of a White Christmas" begins, Marne gets up and leaves the cafeteria.

"I don't know," her husband says wearily, getting up to follow her. "She takes things too hard."

"He's got her a Cuisinart for Christmas," Alice's husband confides.

"She doesn't have anybody to cook for," Alice says sadly.

On Christmas morning, the sun shines on a dusting of snow on the tops of all the surrounding mountains, from a storm that passed through in the night. The Dirkheimers and Hootsteins are waving to everyone as they start out to the airport. Hymen is wearing swimming goggles to look like a World War I aviator.

"Can't Jews eat turkey?" Marne asks Alice. "There's nothing religious about that, is there?"

"Maybe if they're kosher," Alice suggests doubtfully, as they stroll toward the pool.

"Look," Marne whispers, "the naked ape has a new St. Christopher medal around his neck."

"Santa Claus probably gave it to him," Alice whispers back.

"In his Mercedes," Marne adds, thinking, at least Joe isn't a faggot.

Miss Jensen, already at the pool, is again reading T. S. Eliot, "The Journey of the Magi," in honor of the day which will otherwise go unremarked until the evening feast. She and her friend, who is on her morning ride, have given each other a new freezer for the house they share, which was installed before they left for their Death Valley holiday.

Then at dawn we came down to a temperate valley
Wet, below the snow line, smelling of vegetation

Miss Jensen lifts her eyes to the mountains and thinks, in such a place as this miracles can be expected but are not. She finds it curious that so many of the places Indians chose to live have been left essentially uninhabited by white men. Here the Indians wintered in the valley and retreated into the mountains to escape the heat of summer, a sensible arrangement requiring neither furnace nor air-conditioner, to say nothing of a freezer.

All that was a long time ago, I remember

Ginter and Faymoor are joining their wives. Foregoing their golf game is as close to a religious gesture as they will make. They all discuss not phoning their children in elaborate agreement over not being able to get through, over getting through and being handed over to a grandchild too young to talk.

"We'd just make them all jealous," Marne concludes, taking off her robe and stretching out in the sun.

The others study her for gooseflesh. The sun won't really be warm enough for such gestures for another hour.

"At breakfast I heard a woman say she missed cooking Christmas dinner!" Alice offers for laughs.

"I'm going to bust out crying tonight when I don't get to saw away at my very own bird. You know, I don't think I've ever tasted *hot* turkey," Faymoor offers to help the mood along.

"What I think I dislike most about Christmas," Ginter announces in a loud voice, "is that it exists."

"But does it?" the friendly non-lifeguard calls over to him.

Miss Jensen puts down her book and makes slow preparations for her morning swim, involving ear plugs, cap, goggles, and nose clip. This morning, because Hymen isn't there drowning in the way of each turn at the shallow end, she has decided to do a hundred rather than her usual fifty lengths. Since everything today will seem twice as long, she can be willfully cooperative.

"My God," Marne says at Miss Jensen's seventy-fifth turn, "she must be training for the senior Olympics."

The ranch guests going to the inn for dinner have so smartly turned themselves out for the assault on their wealthier neighbors that they hardly recognize their pool and cafeteria companions. Both Marne Alice are in long dresses, their husbands in ties to match. Miss Jensen is in a black pantsuit, her friend is in white, and the non-lifeguard, who is escorting them, wears a crested jacket.

"He must be a good ten years younger than they are," Marne comments.

"They're probably paying for his dinner," Faymoor suggests.

"Mr. Mercedes is, I'll bet," Alice says.

Mr. Mercedes certainly greets the threesome like a proper host, though he hasn't bothered to put on a tie for the occasion. He's got on a black turtleneck, which makes him look faintly religious. In the crowded bar, he has managed to reserve a table, while the Faymoors and Ginters must choose between standing for a drink and having it in the dining room.

"What it costs you to be one of the cattle!" Ginter complains.

"No room at the inn," Alice shouts gaily.

Miss Jensen is helped into her chair, the poem still in her head.

> *We returned to our places, these Kingdoms*
> *But no longer at ease here, in the old dispensation*

Heterosexuality rather than Christianity is the surviving religion here; and she feels, even in the company of these brothers, uncomfortably compromised by it. Briefly she envies the flight of the Jews into the Grand Canyon. Her friend will enjoy the evening as merely exotic. Since Miss Jensen lost her first friend to a combination of fear and boredom, she accepts compromise in defense against such enemies.

In the middle of their first drink, which Mr. Mercedes has ordered by brand, the waiter hands the non-lifeguard a message.

"The little fart!" he cries. "What did he have to do that for?"

"What is it? What's happened?"

"He's crashed that shitty little crate into the salt flats and killed them all!"

The non-lifeguard covers his face and weeps.

No one at the table moves or speaks.

"Who?" someone at the next table asks.

"Sky King?" someone else asks.

"I think we'd better go in to dinner," Miss Jensen says. "Thank you for the drink."

"I'm terribly sorry," Miss Jensen's friend says, laying a light hand on the shoulder of the sobbing man.

Miss Jensen takes her arm to urge her away.

"We should never get mixed up with people like that," Miss Jensen whispers, avoiding the questioning faces of the Ginters and the Faymoors.

"He's your friend, not mine!"

"Maybe we could get their table," Marne suggests.

"But what's happened?" Alice asks.

"Air crash," someone says. "Bunch of people killed."

"Sky King," someone else adds.

Mr. Mercedes has also left the table and is moving quickly through the crowd, answering nobody's questions.

A waiter is trying to get the unhappy and now solitary man to move.

"Come on, hey? It's Christmas, you know. A lot of people here want to be happy. Come on. You can go out through the back here."

Finally he is persuaded to go.

"I feel really faint," Marne says, sitting down at the vacated table.

"They didn't even want to see the Grand Canyon," Ginter says quietly. "They just wanted to avoid . . . this."

"Christmas," Alice says.

"I want to say something," Faymoor announces. "I don't mean to sound hard or anything, but this is our holiday, and we should go on enjoying it, you know?"

"I think maybe we'd better call home," Marne says. "If it's on the news and they don't release names . . . "

"Right after dinner," her husband agrees.

In the morning they are all, except the non-lifeguard, gathered in a crowd at Badwater, the lowest point in the valley, two-hundred-eighty feet below sea level, a sign marking where sea level is on a cliff far above their heads. A large flattop truck and a crane are parked waiting, as the crowd is waiting, for a helicopter to come back from the salt flats with the first fragments of the wreck.

"They got the bodies out last night," someone is explaining.

A child says, "Take a picture of the truck, Daddy."

"It's just a truck. This is the lowest place on the continent. Do you realize that? See, that's sea level way up there."

"I want a picture of the truck."

"Maureen said they had meatloaf," Marne is saying to Alice.

"All you had to do was look at that crate to know it wasn't safe," Ginter is saying to Faymoor. "And the pilot was a drunk. All you had to do was look at him . . ."

"I want to apologize about last night," Mr. Mercedes was saying to a reluctant Miss Jensen and her friend. "They were good friends. It was a terrible shock for him."

His next words are obscured by the sound of the helicopter, which approaches across the mudflats of Badwater like a great bird of prey, its catch part of the fuselage. As it comes to earth, the wind envelops the crowd in a sudden cloud of dust, as if a great conjurer had decided to make them all disappear; but when the fragile dust settles again, they are all still there, watching and talking.

A Perfectly Nice Man

"I'M SORRY I'M late, darling," Virginia said, having to pick up and embrace three-year-old Clarissa before she could kiss Katherine hello. "My last patient needed not only a new crown but some stitches for a broken heart. Why do people persist in marriage?"

"Your coat's cold," Clarissa observed soberly.

"So's my nose," Virginia said, burying it in the child's neck. "It's past your bath time and your story time, and I've probably ruined dinner."

"No," Katherine said. "We're not eating until seven-thirty. We're having a guest."

"Who?"

"Daddy's new friend," Clarissa said. "And I get to stay up until she comes."

"Really?"

"She said she needed to talk with us," Katherine explained. "She sounded all right on the phone. Well, a little nervous but not at all hostile. I thought, perhaps we owe her that much?"

"Or him?" Virginia wondered.

"Oh, if him, I suppose I should have said no," Katherine decided. "People who don't even want to marry him think this is odd enough."

"Odd about him?"

"Even he thinks it's odd about him," Katherine said.

"Men have an exaggerated sense of responsibility in the most peculiar directions," Virginia said. "We can tell her he's a perfectly nice man, can't we?" She was now addressing the child.

"Daddy said I didn't know who was my mommie," Clarissa said.

"Oh?"

"I have two mommies. Will Elizabeth be my mommie, too?"

"She just might," Virginia said. "What a lucky kid that would make you."

"Would she come to live with us then?" Clarissa asked.

"Sounds to me as if she wants to live with Daddy," Virginia said.

"So did you, at first," Clarissa observed.

Both women laughed.

"Your bath!" Virginia ordered and carried the child up the stairs while Katherine returned to the kitchen to attend to dinner.

Clarissa was on the couch in her pajamas, working a pop-up book of *Alice in Wonderland* with Virginia, when the doorbell rang.

"I'll get that," Katherine called from the kitchen.

Elizabeth, in a fur-collared coat, stood in the doorway, offering freesias.

"Did he tell you to bring them?" Katherine asked, smiling.

"He said we all three liked them," Elizabeth answered. "But don't most women?"

"I'm Katherine," Katherine said, "wife number one."

"And I'm Virginia, wife number two," Virginia said, standing in the hall.

"And I'm Elizabeth, as yet unnumbered," Elizabeth said. "And you're Clarissa."

Clarissa nodded, using one of Virginia's legs as a prop for leaning against or perhaps hiding behind.

Elizabeth was dressed, as the other two women were, in very well cut trousers and an expensive blouse, modestly provocative. And she was about their age, thirty. The three did not so much look alike as share a type, all about the same height, five feet seven inches or so (he said he was six feet tall but was, in fact, five feet ten and a half), slightly but well proportioned, with silky, well cut hair and intelligent faces. They were all competent, assured women who intimidated only unconsciously.

Virginia poured three drinks and a small glass of milk for Clarissa, who was allowed to pass the nuts and have one or two before Katherine took her off to bed.

"She looks like her father," Elizabeth observed.

"Yes, she has his lovely eyes," Virginia agreed.

"He doesn't know I'm here," Elizabeth confessed. "Oh, I intend to tell him. I just didn't want it to be a question, you see?"

"He did think it a mistake that Katherine and I ever met. We didn't, of course, until after I'd married him. I didn't know he was married until quite a while after he and I met."

"He was a patient of yours?" Elizabeth asked.

"Yes."

"He's been quite open with me about both of you from the beginning, but we met in therapy, of course, and that does make such a difference."

"Does it?" Virginia asked. "I've never been in therapy."

"Haven't you?" Elizabeth asked, surprised. "I would have thought both of you might have considered it."

"He and I?"

"No, you and Katherine."

"We felt very uncomplicated about it," Virginia said, "once it happened. It was such an obvious solution."

"For him?"

"Well, no, not for him, of course. Therapy was a thing for him to consider."

Katherine came back into the room. "Well, now we can be grown-ups."

"She looks like her father," Elizabeth observed again.

"She has his lovely eyes," it was Katherine's turn to reply.

"I don't suppose a meeting like this could have happened before the women's movement," Elizabeth said.

"Probably not," Katherine agreed. "I'm not sure Virginia and I could have happened before the women's movement. We might not have known what to do."

"He tries not to be antagonistic about feminism," Elizabeth said.

"Oh, he's always been quite good about the politics. He didn't resent my career," Virginia offered.

"He was quite proud of marrying a dentist," Katherine said. "I think he used to think I wasn't liberated enough."

"He doesn't think that now," Elizabeth said.

"I suppose not," Katherine agreed.

"The hardest thing for him has been facing . . . the sexual implications. He has felt . . . unmanned."

"He's put it more strongly than that in the past," Virginia said.

"Men's sexuality is so much more fragile than ours," Elizabeth said.

"Shall we have dinner?" Katherine suggested.

"He said you were a very good cook," Elizabeth said to Katherine.

"Most of this dinner is Virginia's. I got it out of the freezer," Katherine explained. "I've gone back to school, and I don't have that much time."

"I cook in binges," Virginia said, pouring the wine.

"At first he said he thought the whole thing was some kind of crazy revenge," Elizabeth said.

"At first there might have been that element in it," Virginia admitted. "Katherine was six months' pregnant when he left her, and she felt horribly deserted. I didn't know he was going to be a father until after Clarissa was born. Then I felt I'd betrayed her, too, though I hadn't known anything about it."

"He said he should have told you," Elizabeth said, "but he was very much in love and was afraid of losing you. He said there was never any question of his not supporting Katherine and Clarissa."

"No, I make perfectly good money," Virginia said. "There's no question of his supporting them now, if that's a problem. He doesn't."

"He says he'd rather he did," Elizabeth said.

"He sees Clarissa whenever he likes," Katherine explained. "He's very good with her. One of the reasons I wanted a baby was knowing he'd be a good sort of father."

"Did you have any reservations about marrying him?" Elizabeth asked Virginia.

"At the time? Only that I so very much wanted to," Virginia said. "There aren't that many marrying men around for women dentists, unless they're sponges, of course. It's flattering when someone is so afraid of losing you he's willing to do something legal about it. It oughtn't to be, but it is."

"But you had other reservations later," Elizabeth said.

"Certainly, his wife and his child."

"Why did he leave you, Katherine?"

"Because he was afraid of losing her. I suppose he thought he'd have what he needed of me anyway, since I was having his child."

"Were you still in love with him?" Elizabeth asked.

"I must have been," Katherine said, "or I couldn't have been quite so unhappy, so desperate. I was desperate."

"He's not difficult to be in love with, after all," Virginia said. "He's a very attractive man."

"He asked me if I was a lesbian," Elizabeth said. "I told him I certainly didn't think so. After all, I was in love with him. He said so had two other women been, in love enough to marry him, but they were both lesbians. And maybe he only attracted lesbians even if they didn't know it themselves. He even suggested I should maybe try making love with another woman before I made up my mind."

There was a pause which neither Katherine nor Virginia attempted to break.

"Did either of you know . . . before?"

Katherine and Virginia looked at each other. Then they said, "No."

"He's even afraid he may turn women into lesbians," Elizabeth said.

Both Virginia and Katherine laughed, but not unkindly.

"Is that possible?" Elizabeth asked.

"Is that one of *your* reservations?" Katherine asked.

"It seemed crazy," Elizabeth said, "but . . . "

Again the two hostesses waited.

"I know this probably sounds very unliberated and old-fashioned and maybe even prejudiced, but I don't think I could stand being a lesbian, finding out I'm a lesbian; and if there's something in him that makes a woman . . . How can either of you stand to be together instead of with him?"

"But you don't know you're a lesbian until you fall in love," Katherine said, "and then it's quite natural to want to be together with the person you love."

"What's happening to me is so peculiar. The more sure I am I'm in love with him, the more obsessively I read everything I can about what it is to be a lesbian. It's almost as if I *had* fallen in love with a woman, and that's absurd."

"I don't really think there's anything peculiar about him," Katherine said.

"One is just so naturally drawn, so able to identify with another woman," Virginia said. "When I finally met Katherine, what he wanted and needed just seemed too ridiculous."

"But it was you he wanted," Elizabeth protested.

"At Katherine's and Clarissa's expense, and what was I, after all, but just another woman."

"A liberated woman," Katherine said.

"Not then, I wasn't," Virginia said.

"I didn't feel naturally drawn to either of you," Elizabeth protested. "I wasn't even curious at first. But he's so obsessed with you still, so afraid of being betrayed again, and I thought, I've got to help him somehow, reassure him, understand enough to let him know, as you say, that there's nothing peculiar about him . . . or me."

"I'm sure there isn't," Katherine said reassuringly and reached out to take Elizabeth's hand.

Virginia got up to clear the table.

"Mom!" came the imperious and sleepy voice of Clarissa.

"I'll go," Virginia said.

"But I don't think you mean what I want you to mean," Elizabeth said.

"Perhaps not," Katherine admitted.

"He said he never should have left you. It was absolutely wrong; and if he ever did marry again, it would be because he wanted to make that commitment, but what if his next wife found out she didn't want him, the way Virginia did?"

"I guess anyone takes that risk," Katherine said.

"Do you think I should marry him?" Elizabeth asked.

Katherine kept Elizabeth's hand, and her eyes met Elizabeth's beseeching, but she didn't answer.

"You *do* think there's something wrong with him."

"No, I honestly don't. He's a perfectly nice man. It's just that I sometimes think that isn't good enough, not now when there are other options."

"What other options?"

"You have a job, don't you?"

"I teach at the university, as he does."

"Then you can support yourself."

"That's not always as glamorous as it sounds."

"Neither is marriage," Katherine said.

"Is this?" Elizabeth asked, looking around her, just as Virginia came back into the room.

"It's not nearly as hard as some people try to make it sound."

"Clarissa wanted to know if her new mother was still here."

"Oh my," Elizabeth said.

"Before you came, she wanted to know, if you married her father, would you be another mother and move in here."

Elizabeth laughed and then said, "Oh, God, that's just what he wants to know!"

They took their coffee back into the living room.

"It must be marvelous to be a dentist. At least during the day you can keep people from telling you all their troubles," Elizabeth said.

"That's not as easy as it looks," Virginia said.

"He says you're the best dentist he ever went to. He hates his dentist now."

"I used to be so glad he wasn't like so many men who fell in love with their students," Katherine said.

"Maybe he'd be better off," Elizabeth said in mock gloom. "He says he isn't threatened by my having published more than he has. He had two wives and a baby while I was simply getting on with it; but does he mean it? Does he really know?"

"We're all reading new lines, aren't we?" Virginia asked.

"But if finally none of us marries them, what will they do?" Elizabeth asked.

"I can hardly imagine that," Katherine said.

"You can't imagine what they'll do?"

"No, women saying 'no,' all of them. We can simply consider ourselves, for instance," Katherine said.

"Briefly anyway," Virginia said. "Did you come partly to see if you were at all like us?"

"I suppose so," Elizabeth said.

"Are you?"

"Well, I'm not surprised by you . . . and very surprised not to be."

"Are you sorry to have married him?" Virginia asked Katherine.

"I could hardly be. There's Clarissa, after all, and you. Are you?" she asked in return.

"Not now," Virginia said, "having been able to repair the damage."

"And everyone knows," Elizabeth said, "that you did have the choice."

"Yes," Virginia agreed, "there's that."

"But I felt I didn't have any choice," Katherine said. "That part of it humiliated me."

"Elizabeth is making a distinction," Virginia said, "between what everyone knows and what each of us knows. I shared your private humiliation, of course. All women must."

"Why?" Elizabeth demanded.

"Not to believe sufficiently in one's own value," Virginia explained.

"But he doesn't believe sufficiently in his own value either," Elizabeth said. "He doesn't even quite believe he's a man."

"I never doubted I was a woman," Katherine said.

"That's smug," Elizabeth said, "because you have a child."

"So does he," Katherine replied.

"But he was too immature to deal with it; he says so himself. Don't you feel at all sorry for him?"

"Yes," said Katherine.

"Of course," Virginia agreed.

"He's been terribly hurt. He's been damaged," Elizabeth said.

"Does that make him more or less attractive, do you think?" Virginia asked.

"Well, damn it, less, of course," Elizabeth shouted. "And whose fault is that?"

Neither of the other two women answered.

"He's not just second, he's third-hand goods," Elizabeth said.

"Are women going to begin to care about men's virginity?" Katherine asked. "How extraordinary!"

"Why did you go into therapy?" Virginia asked.

"I hardly remember," Elizabeth said. "I've been so caught up with his problems since the beginning. The very first night of group, he said I somehow reminded him of his wives . . . "

"Perhaps that is why you went," Katherine suggested.

"You think I'd be crazy to marry him, don't you?" Elizabeth demanded.

"Why should we?" Virginia asked. "We both did."

"That's not a reassuring point," Elizabeth said.

"You find us unsatisfactory," Katherine said, in apology.

"Exactly not," Elizabeth said sadly. "I want someone to advise me . . . to make a mistake. Why should you?"

"Why indeed?" Virginia asked.

They embraced warmly before Elizabeth left.

"Perhaps I might come again?" she asked at the door.

"Of course," Katherine said.

After the door closed, Katherine and Virginia embraced.

"He'd be so much happier, for a while anyway, if he married again," Katherine said.

"Of course he would," Virginia agreed, with some sympathy for him in her voice. "But we couldn't encourage a perfectly nice woman like Elizabeth   "

"That's the problem, isn't it?" Katherine said. "That's just it."

"She'll marry him anyway," Virginia predicted, "briefly."

"And have a child?" Katherine asked.

"And fall in love with his next wife," Virginia went on.

"There really isn't anything peculiar about him," Katherine said. "I'm sorry he doesn't like his dentist."

"He should never have married you."

"No, he shouldn't," Virginia agreed. "Then at least I could still be taking care of his teeth."

Barring that, they went up together to look in on his richly mothered child, sleeping soundly, before they went to their own welcoming bed.

Night Call

THE PHONE RANG along the nerves of a dream, finally breaking Eva's sleep. Next to her Christine turned, disturbed. Eva put a firm hand on her hip.

"I'll get it."

But she waited for the phone to ring once more to give herself time to be awake, to squint at the luminous face of the clock. It was three-thirty in the morning.

"Hello?"

"Hello. Is it Eva?"

The hollow silence around the voice alerted Eva to long distance, and the voice itself was familiar, but not familiar enough to be identified quickly. "Yes, it's Eva."

"It's Joyce," the voice said. "How are you?"

Joyce? The Joyce who belonged to that voice was no more than an acquaintance, a friend of a friend; and as far as Eva could remember, still not clearly awake, she was in Europe this year or was supposed to be.

"Joyce Carlyle," the voice encouraged.

"Where are you?" Eva asked.

"In Coventry."

"England?"

"That's right. How are you?"

She didn't sound as if she had been drinking. In fact, the voice was pleasant and impersonal enough to be offering a neighborly good morning. Not surprising perhaps. It must be morning in England. It must be nearly noon.

"What's the trouble, Joyce?"

"I was wondering if you could do me a favor."

"If I can."

Christine had sat up and turned on the low bedside lamp.

"It's Arlene," Joyce said.

"Arlene?"

"The girl I introduced you to that day at lunch. Don't you remember? And you met her again a couple of months ago at a dinner party, at the Stephens, I think."

"Oh yes," Eva said, immediately depressed and irritated by the memory. "I remember."

"Well, I'm worried about her. I wonder if you could telephone her and just see if she's all right."

"Now?"

"If you wouldn't mind."

"Do you know what time it is?" Eva asked. "Here, I mean?"

"I guess it's pretty late, is it?"

"Three-thirty in the morning."

"But I'm afraid she might do something, do you see?"

"Why? What's the trouble?"

"Well, I had this letter, and she was so unhappy."

"But she must have written that days ago, Joyce."

"Yes. I telephoned her, though."

"How long ago?"

"Oh, I don't know. A couple of hours maybe, maybe a little longer. She hung up on me, and I'm so worried about her, Eva. She wanted to come over here. I couldn't let her do that. I tried to explain to her. There's this man I've been expecting. I'm going to meet his boat next week; so, you see, it would be just impossible. If you could just explain it to her, Eva."

"I don't even know the girl," Eva protested. "I can't really telephone at this hour in the morning. What if I got her husband?"

"But I'm afraid she may kill herself. If you could just tell her that I do love her, that I love her very much, but I simply couldn't live like *that.*"

Christine was sitting on the edge of the bed, lighting cigarettes for them both, her skin blankly pale in the soft light, nearly the color of her hair, her fine hands awkward with sleep.

"It doesn't seem to me a very helpful message at this hour in the morning," Eva said sharply.

"But, what if . . ."

"Look, I will telephone first thing tomorrow. I'll see what I can do then, all right?"

"You were the only person I could think of who might . . ."

"I hardly know the girl," Eva insisted. "I'll phone in the morning."

"She said she could talk to you; she was sure she could. I made her promise me she wouldn't do anything without talking to you."

"I'll do what I can tomorrow. Do you want me to write to you?"

"If you would."

"What's your address?"

Christine reached for paper and pencil and copied the address as Eva repeated it. The expression on her strong and aging face, which other people so often called serene, Eva recognized as resigned, and she resented Joyce Carlyle and Arlene and their silly melodrama.

"I'll let you know then," Eva said.

"Just tell her . . ."

"I will," Eva interrupted, not trusting herself to hear the message again without losing her temper.

"Thanks. I knew I could count on you."

Why? Eva thought, as she put the phone down. Joyce hardly knew her. But she did know why, and there was no point in resenting it.

"What's the matter?" Christine asked.

"I don't really know," Eva said, "but we're not going to lose any more sleep over it. Put out your cigarette."

"Why would Joyce Carlyle call you?"

"Because she's been having an affair with a girl who is threatening to kill herself."

"What does she expect you do to about it?"

"Telephone her and inquire after her health. Well, she's either dead or asleep by now. We're not going to do anything about it until morning. I'll think about it then."

Christine butted her cigarette and turned out the light.

"I'm sorry, darling," Eva said, settling Christine into the curve of her younger, longer body.

"It's not your fault."

"Let's sleep."

Neither of them did at once. They lay still in the darkness. Eva watched the flash of the lighthouse beacon illuminate the wallpaper, heard the morning foghorns begin, smelled the fragrance of dawn. In Coventry. Eleven-thirty Sunday morning there; she should have been in church! Even Eva went to church in Coventry. She couldn't imagine anyone's killing herself for Joyce Carlyle, a woman always peddling backward, out of marriage, out of motherhood, back to the adolescence she imagined she'd missed, back to groping college boys in the back seats of cars or to "older men" no older than she. It hadn't occurred to Eva that Joyce was having an affair with Arlene until that dinner party in September. Then she found the revelation simply distasteful, had not turned her imagination to it at all. Well, perhaps she had for a moment, just before she and Christine had left the party.

Arlene, inexcusably drunk at an otherwise sober occasion, had been assertive and argumentative all evening. When she was gradually closed out of the conversation, not so much from rudeness as from concern the other guests felt for her suffering husband, she followed the hostess into the kitchen and obviously embarrassed her with miserable confessions. Christine had not encountered Arlene all evening, and Eva had avoided her too, as much as she could; but as she crossed the room to get their coats, Arlene had taken hold of her wrist, stared up at her through unfocusing tears, and said:

"What am I going to do? I can't live without Joyce."

Eva was angry with her, at the damage she had done to the party and to her husband. And she was repelled by the slackness of mouth, the puppet awkwardness of arms and legs, the more because Arlene could have been a beautiful young woman, was beautiful, in fact. Eva could see what was all but canceled by self-indulgence and self-pity.

"I've got to talk to somebody. I can't stand it," Arlene said.

"Yes you can," Eva answered and found she had cupped the back of Arlene's unsteady head with her hand.

"You won't talk to me."

"Phone me if you need me," Eva answered and then moved away.

"I'm so sorry," the hostess was saying as she handed Eva her own and Christine's coats. "She said she wanted to meet you. I had no idea . . . I'm so sorry, Eva, to get you into this."

"You didn't get anybody into anything," Eva said.

"I never would have introduced you," the hostess went on.

"I've already met her," Eva said. "I met her last spring. She's no problem to me. Don't worry about it. It was a lovely party."

"That poor young man," Christine said, once they were in the car.

They had talked about him, the young husband in his dignified endurance, on the way home. Eva did not mention the exchange between herself and Arlene, reluctant to distress Christine with it, in some part of her guilty about it as well. There was in Eva something left of her own early unsettled life, things she regretted rather than missed. Still, sometimes the decorum, the sense of social responsibility Christine had taught her in the last twelve years were constricting. It would have been inhuman, as well as sensible, not to have laid a hand on that head. Arlene had not telephoned, and Eva forgot her.

Breakfast was always a silent but not an unpleasant meal. Christine usually woke earlier than Eva and therefore fixed the coffee and poured the juice, waiting to cook whatever they wanted until she heard Eva get up. They were having a second cup of coffee before Christine spoke.

"What are you going to do?"

"About what?" Eva asked, turning from contemplating the dry leaves on the witch hazel, which Christine would soon want to cut off.

"About that girl."

Eva was puzzled.

"The phone call last night."

"I'd forgotten all about it," Eva said.

"I wish I hadn't reminded you."

Eva turned again to the winter garden out beyond the rain-soaked glass, but she did not see it now. As she recalled the conversation with Joyce, she felt defensive and resentful. This was to have been a quiet day with two old and comfortable friends coming for dinner.

"I am supposed to telephone a girl I don't know and deliver a message that Joyce loves her very much but couldn't possibly consider living like *that*."

"Like what?"

"Like *this*," Eva said.

"I don't know how you can."

"Apparently Joyce is meeting a man, and so she can't meet Arlene."

"Was Arlene planning to join her? How could she? She's still living with her husband, isn't she? Doesn't she have children?"

"I think so. It's all very unlikely."

"I don't know why people can't leave you alone."

"Well, there's nothing I can do, is there? I can't telephone. What would I say?"

"Is Joyce really worried that she might kill herself?"

"I suppose so. Otherwise, I don't know why she would have telephoned. Maybe . . . "

"Maybe what?"

"Maybe she just wanted somebody else to take over. 'I'm tired of her now, so you cope.' "

"What if Arlene really is in trouble?" Christine asked.

"Yes, what if she is? What if she doesn't really have anyone to talk to?"

"I might call the Stephens," Christine suggested. "They're obviously friends of hers."

"What would you say?"

"Well, I could say a mutual friend was worried about her. I could simply say we didn't know what we could do, not knowing her."

"Why should you get involved?" Eva demanded.

"Better I than you."

Christine called the Stephens, but she didn't get much information. They had seen as little of Arlene and her husband as they could since the night of the dinner party, but they were concerned. They suggested the name of a closer friend, a woman Christine and Eva knew because she had bought paintings from their gallery.

"Are you going to call her?" Eva asked.

"Yes. If we can just be sure somebody who does know her is alerted, then we can forget it."

Eva went to the kitchen to make the casserole, so that she wouldn't simply stand in the study, listening and wanting to prompt. Christine was very good at saying no more than she intended. Eva could not deal with any problem except directly. She was stirring the cream sauce when Christine came in to explain what had happened.

"I think that will do it," she said. "She'll telephone Arlene."

"Did you have to explain much?"

"No. She said she knew Arlene had been depressed earlier in the fall, but she'd been in much better spirits lately. A nice woman. She said, 'Actually I've been so depressed myself lately, I haven't been paying attention to anyone else.' But she will now. So I think that's all we have to do. Who's making the pie tonight?"

"I am, as soon as I finish this."

They were sitting in front of the fire with brandy, talking about the possibility of a winter holiday somewhere in the sun. It was not yet eleven o'clock, but Christine looked tired.

"It's been a hard fall for everyone," Dore said, sitting on the floor and leaning against Christine's footstool. "And now Christmas. Mary and I think we'll just hang a sign in the window and take off for two weeks in early February."

"Ten days anyway," Mary said, the more cautious of the two. "Why don't you both come with us?"

"We have two shows in February," Christine said. "And Eva has a show of her own coming up in the east in early April."

"Still," Eva said, "we might be able to juggle dates."

She liked the idea of getting Christine away from business into the sun, and traveling with Dore and Mary was always a good idea. Dore was adventuresome and tireless, a companion for the long walks Eva liked to take, and as enthusiastic for the historical sightseeing that Christine enjoyed. Mary was content with any plan that used up Dore's energy in the safe company of friends; and when she was content, she was comic. Christine never laughed the way she did at Mary, with Mary, except on such holidays.

"All we have to do is keep Dore from getting us involved in five excursions a day," Mary said. "A winter holiday is supposed to be a rest."

"You can rest. Christine and I . . ."

The phone rang. Christine looked at Eva and started to get up.

"I'll get it," Eva said.

"Should you?"

"I don't see why not."

As Eva went to the study, she heard Mary ask, "You're not still being bothered by crank calls, are you?"

Eva knew they would go on to talk about unlisted phones and other impractical solutions.

"Hello?"

"Hi."

Eva knew it was Arlene and could not pretend she didn't. "How are you?"

"Not bad. Better. You said to telephone you; so I am. I sound like I've got a cold, but I don't. I sound like I'm drunk, but I'm not very. I thought maybe you could give me some addresses, you know?"

"Addresses?"

"Well, it's all broken up with Joyce. I'm through there, and I need somebody else. You know all these women, have all these woman. I thought maybe you'd give me an address or two, or a telephone number or something. I don't know how to go about finding them. You have all these women. How do you find them anyway?"

"I don't know what you're talking about," Eva said.

"Sure you do. My God! I mean, all those models. Those pictures were real, baby. Anyway, everybody knows it. You've got women, lots of them."

"You're talking nonsense," Eva said, tempted to hang up but unwilling to because there was such angry sorrow in that drunken voice.

"Well, so I shouldn't ask for private stock. What about some bars? Which are the good bars?"

"I don't know," Eva said. "I've never been to one."

"No kidding? Well, so you don't need to. I do. You've got to understand that, you of all people. How do you meet women? How do you find them? I'm through with the straight ones. All those months. All that work. And then what have you got? Nothing. Where are the gay women in this town? That's what I have to know."

"Haven't you had enough?" Eva asked.

"I've never had enough. Why don't you hang up on me? Why are you still talking to me?"

"I don't know," Eva said. "Why am I?"

"Because you're a humanitarian. You feel sorry for me, don't you? You don't have to, though. I'm really fine. Last night wasn't so good, but today . . ."

Eva stood, then sat down, finally smoked a cigarette, while Arlene rambled and begged and clowned and sometimes cried. She talked about her beautiful kids, about her dubious but tolerant husband, about Joyce, about drinking, about women. Sometimes she was incoherently obscene, sometimes sharply, self-critically witty. Finally, after nearly half an hour had passed, Eva decided that she was telling the truth: she was all right, that is, alive, and willing to live.

"Can I call you again?" Arlene asked.

"All right, but not after ten in the evening and not before ten in the morning and preferably when you're a little less drunk than you are now."

"Tough guy."

"That's right."

"I'll pose for you," Arlene offered.

"Thanks just the same. As you've already pointed out, I have all these women."

"I'm not bad," Arlene said. "Not bad at all."

"You could be perfectly lovely. Good night."

"Good night, and thanks."

Eva stood for a moment then before she went back into the living room. She had to recover her resentment before she could explain. Or at least she had to assign Arlene to appropriate categories: emotionally disturbed? hopelessly self-indulgent? childish? As everyone is at moments, through hours, even weeks. Dangerous. Arlene was dangerous, just as Eva had been once in fact and was now in image. With all that willful appetite, sourced in loneliness and destructiveness perhaps or in sheer energy. And if Eva could forget everything that mattered to her—her work, her sanity, Christine, and yes, even Arlene herself—she would lie down with that need in herself, make use, make violent, beautiful use of what was offered her. Why? Because it would be such a relief to put herself down like that, immediately, with new urgency and nothing else. There was no point in feeling guilty. But Eva went back into the living room with an energy she did not know how to use.

"Who was it?" Christine asked.

"Arlene."

"I told them about last night's call," Christine said. "How was she?"

"Drunk. In pain. She wanted to know if I could give her some addresses. She wanted to know about the bars. She wanted to know where she could find gay women in this town."

"Why didn't you ask her over?" Dore suggested wryly.

"Is she all right?" Christine insisted.

"Yes, darling, she's all right. Life force up full volume."

"Are you going to have to cope with her?"

"I don't know. Maybe occasionally."

"Why?" Mary asked. "Why should you?"

"Because she's there," Dore answered, watching Eva with some candor.

"Which one of us hasn't wanted to say things like that?" Eva asked. "Which one of us hasn't felt like that?"

"It's an old argument," Mary said, "you and Dore on one side, Christine and I on the other."

"Not always," Christine said.

"The real difference between Eva and me," Dore said, "is that she thinks sex has to have redeeming social significance. All I ever want is a simple roll in the hay. Then Mary and I can have a good fight about it, and that's that."

"What you mean is," Eva said, grinning, "that you've stopped rationalizing."

"No, I don't. If your paintings were simply erotic, you wouldn't create such a ruckus."

"That's the third time Christine has yawned through her ears," Mary said.

Christine didn't apologize. She got up with Mary and Dore to find their coats.

"They'll have a fight on the way home," Eva said, "about why Mary always stops a conversation just when it gets interesting."

"Mary can blame me," Christine said. "Was it interesting?"

"You don't like it when Dore baits me."

"Dore oversimplifies, about herself as well."

"Sometimes that's clarifying," Eva said.

"She's not going to make us have a fight about Arlene," Christine said firmly.

"Not tonight."

"Not ever."

Eva, confined in Christine's arms, heard Joyce's voice saying, "Tell her that I do love her, that I love her very much, but I simply couldn't live like *that*." Eva stretched and reached under the bedside table, taking the phone jack out of the wall.

"The proverbial barn door," Christine said.

Eva saw Arlene and Joyce riding their stolen horses into the melodramatic night, the lighthouse flashing its steady warning into this quiet room. She turned and held Christine, who was already asleep.

Essays

Sexuality in Literature

I HAVE BEEN out of the academy long enough not to make a fetish of defining terms; but the word *erotic*, in the dictionary simply "pertaining to sexual love," carries with it for a great many people pejorative meanings as well. Erotic literature is expected to be sexually arousing and therefore, at least to some, "obscene," offensive to modesty or decency. Erotic language is "dirty" language. Though there are obvious institutions to blame for our prudery and squeamishness about sexuality, even without centuries of repression by the church, there are fundamental ambiguities in our nature and condition which would never allow us the innocent and simple sexual pleasure we can think is out there beyond all the negative morality. It is not my purpose here to discuss the complexities of relationship between our sexual and mortal natures but only to suggest that a body we know is designed to die will never be a simple plaything, nor will the language we use to express our sexuality ever be without that irony. As if that weren't problem enough, much of what is sexual has nothing to do with love or even, for both or all parties, pleasure. It is perfectly clear why erotic language so often borrows images from the hunt, why Kate Millett's title *Sexual Politics* has become one of our defining phrases. A language adequate to express our sexual experience must be able to describe negotiations far more complex than the entrance of penis or finger into vagina, and it will arouse pity and terror as well as pleasure in its readers if it says anything real about that experience.

For many writers the question of erotic acts and language is confined to personal taste or inhibition. In poetry, in poetic or autobiographical prose, the writer has the hard but clear job of establishing her own preferences and taboos in a language graphically or metaphorically accurate and appealing at least to her.

Adrienne Rich, therefore, in *The Dream of a Common Language*, draws very particularly on her own experience in loving another woman. In "Twenty-one Love Poems" there is only one, "The Floating Poem, Unnumbered," which focuses on the sexual. Even in it, she avoids the names of most sexual parts of the body. There are the "half-curled frond/of the fiddlehead fern" and the "rose-wet cave" instead. Monique Wittig, on the other hand, in *The Lesbian Body*, fills the pages of a book with the parts of the female body with the accuracy of a medical student and the passion of a devouring lover until every bone, muscle, nerve, gland, secretion is eroticized in a dissection which goes on and on in sexual frenzy. While Adrienne Rich is choosing to love "for once/with all my intelligence" and therefore rejects as much as she can the obsessive, the guilt-ridden, the fearful, or holds them at the arm's length of reason to understand and control them, Monique Wittig enters the experience and allows all the Catholic energy of disgust, the cannibal urgency as well as the tenderness and wonder simply to be. Between these extremes are a number of autobiographical writers in the process of explaining their sexual experience as vividly as they can. Kate Millett in *Sita* can be extravagantly romantic, biblical in language rhythms, and come down hard with a political fist. "I am her cunt and against my will I tell her so, slavish, owned, devoted, open, a thing to be used."

Though all three of these writers are lesbian and writing about sexual experience between women, only Adrienne Rich makes an attempt to describe and live in terms of a relationship between two equals. For her, therefore, the problem of erotic language is severe, because political connotations of sexual nouns like *cunt* are alien to that experience. Both Monique Wittig and Kate Millett are describing relationships in which there is a struggle for power not only between the lovers but in each to be at the same time slavish worshiper and devourer, as if the lover were a manifestation of what we call holy and therefore eat. They have rich sources of erotic behavior and language, since so much of myth already incarnates unequal love, the transformation of lover into beast or tree, since all already sexual language carries with it the colors of domination, worship, and death. Yet, of the three, the very spareness of Adrienne Rich's language for "a whole new poetry beginning here" can arouse desire in the mind undivorced from the body, a longing for resolution which is neither union nor death.

It is probably obvious that Adrienne Rich is for me the writer who has something new and important to say, but as a writer I may learn as much from the other two. For the novelist the problem of erotic behavior and language is not one of personal taste or inhibition. Just as a novelist does not give all her characters her own features, needs, moods, so the sexual natures of characters vary, and the novelist who chooses to deal with that aspect of her characters may often be faced with offenses against her own taste and morality, or at least a very hard balance among the requirements of aesthetics and truth must be struck.

There are arguments for avoiding the problem altogether from those who want sexuality denied or at least kept secret. There are arguments for partial censorship for political as well as moral reasons. There are lesbians who see no reason to write anything about male or heterosexual experience. Increasing numbers of women are arguing for censorship of erotic materials which abuse women and children, willing to risk sacrificing freedom to prevent license.

For anyone to deal with even a limited range of sexuality, there is a lot that is exploitative and abusive both in people's fantasies and in their behavior. If we are ever going to understand ourselves as sexual creatures, at least some novelists and biographers, as well as sexologists, are going to have to learn to be accurate about sexual experience, knowing the difference between fantasy and fact, between what ought to be and what is. Knowledge is a collective enterprise. Without it understanding is impossible. Ignorance is too often a murderous vulnerability.

Having decided that what is explicitly sexual is sometimes necessary in my own work, and being the sort of novelist who needs to draw on a range of experience often beyond my own, I am particularly grateful to writers like the three I have mentioned, for they open both ranges of experience and attitudes my own life might not encompass. I have to be equally grateful to the writers Kate Millett so expertly exposed in *Sexual Politics* for giving me some real insight into the abusive violence some men feel toward women; for, given the requirements of my own craft, I may have to be for a while inside such a man's head. There I must be willing to use a language and speak a view that is authentic to him, however offensive it may be to me.

I remember how surprised I was when my first novel was about to be published and I was informed that I could be sued for anything any one of my characters said. "But I often don't agree with what they say," I protested. The lawyer was not interested in the clear distinction I make between my own voice and the voices of my characters. Neither, I have found, are many of my readers. A friend on Galiano tried to defend me to someone protesting the "foul" language in *The Young in One Another's Arms* with, "But Jane doesn't talk like that. It's just her characters." And I hear that it sounds like the sort of defense my brother used when he was three or four years old and always blamed what he had broken, eaten, neglected to eat, on "two bears." Anything I allow to be in my fictional world is something I have to take responsibility for.

Censoring subject matter doesn't seem to be the answer. Pretending self-righteously violent men do not exist will not make them go away. The aggressive man and the masochistic woman are the sexual norms of our society. As clichés they affect real men and women in relationship with each other. Presented uncritically in novels, plays, films, they can reinforce the acceptability of abusive and submissive behavior. Entirely censored, they are given a different sort of freedom to exist in secret, as so much child abuse does.

Morality for the novelist is expressed not so much in the choice of subject matter as in the plot of the narrative, which is perhaps why in our morally bewildered time novelists have often been timid about plot. Who is materially rewarded, emotionally fulfilled, allowed to live, are more powerful judgments than pages of sermonizing. Real propagandists are always strong plot-makers. Dickens, killing innocent children to make his readers guilty enough to reform, is a classic example. There can be both relief and satisfaction in witnessing a system of rewards and punishments we so miss in real life that we have invented heaven and hell as compensations. What sadistic fun Dante had putting all his personal and political enemies through a hell of his own designing, and yet he is never singled out with de Sade as a man of perverse tastes, because Dante was being "moral." Even I, not Catholic, raised in a nominally Christian family in which reason took precedence over systems of rewards and punishments, was so affected by Dante's particularly designed tortures that I had to write his burning sands out of my homosexual heart before I could go on to saner perceptions. I resist strictly moral consequences in my fiction. I so little like to kill people that victims of so severe a judgment begin to build up unnatural amounts of sympathy to resist such character assassination. And so characters should if they are anything but mouthpieces for a point of view. In these morally suspect times, it is as dangerous in fiction as it is in life to make martyrs. I leave my characters so much still alive with so many options left that readers often write to me suggesting sequels in which finally justice is done. They often don't want to reward the characters I would choose or punish those I find most reprehensible.

Resisting judgment in plot is not simply a matter of squeamishness, uncertainty, or lack of responsibility. It is, in my case, resisting mistakes and lies, particularly in the realm of erotic experience. Take a simple example of that kind of lie: men do not respect—that is, marry—women who are sexually generous. Even before the pill, marriage was not the reward of the virtuous nearly as often as it was the result of pregnancy, an entrapment in which men were perceived as the victims and allowed, therefore, some measure of revenge, harsh economic control, rape inside marriage, drunken brutality. Now, as women have greater control over their own bodies and greater economic opportunities for independence, they increasingly fear the entrapment of marriage and understand, as they didn't before, when they had fewer options, that they are the real victims of the institution they have been taught to work so hard to deserve. Fiction that goes on "rewarding" women with marriage serves a morality I find reprehensible. Nevertheless, some of my characters do marry hopefully, with a sense of being rewarded. One is even a virgin (probably frigid). I am trying to write about the real world in which people are often influenced by the silliest of moral teachings, for which I am more interested in understanding than judging them. Marriage does not come at the end of a book or story. There is always time left for irony. My responsibility, as I see it, is not to present the world as it ought to be but as it is. Understanding is an imperfect tool of limited effectiveness in controlling or changing anything, but it can lay before us the options of cynic or lover in terms less distorted than any-thing either Dickens or Dante has offered us.

Dealing with the lies about sexual experience by avoiding obvious devices of plot is easier than dealing with the problems of erotic lan-guage. The vocabulary of sexual love is male ammunition for the an-cient war. Even the medical terms which are used for parts of the female body like *vagina* ("sheath") and *clitoris* (from "to shut or hide") are descriptive only of the male uses of them. Most vulgar terms like *boobs* manage not only to describe female breasts but to suggest some-thing worthless (booby prize) and at the same time dangerous (booby trap). Women use for themselves such terms as *horny* and *jerk off* though neither is descriptive of their own physical experience. There may have been some value at first in taking male vocabulary so that it is no longer something exclusively for their use. A standard defense against all negative slang is the adopting of it by the abused group for positive identity, as has happened with *dyke* and *faggot*. Recently there have also been attempts to make language speak for the female. I read in *Lesbian Tide* a claim that some women have "clit," the female equivalent for "balls." We may find value in words adopted and adap-ted, but they often seem more adequate for those sexual experiences which are as concerned with power as with pleasure, in their excite-ment something offensive. In the mouths of some of my characters as well as in their reveries, such words retain their ambiguity. One of my characters, a writer herself, broods on the limitations of erotic language:

> The problem is that I have no language at all for my body or Rox-anne's body that isn't either derisive or embarrassing. I don't like to write about fingering her ass hole, which immediately becomes per-sonified for me as a belligerently stupid male, a surreal genie, meta-phorical fart emanating from that . . . anus? I think of licorice, which I don't like. We make love without nouns as much as possible, speak in directions instead. 'There.' 'Here?' 'Yes, there.' Adequate for the lovely circumstance of two very present and visible bodies which are wonderfully familiar in fact as well as practice, but a love letter filled with nothing but adverbs is ridiculous. Gertrude Stein tried to invent a new language for love-making, but it was more a code to be cracked than a communication. Imagine the limitation of that when scholars are still debating whether 'cow' means turd or orgasm.

Well, an adequate love poem has been written with adverbs. Here
is one of Phyllis Webb's *Naked Poems:*

> And
> here
> and here and
> here
> and over   and
> over   your mouth.

I am sympathetic with my character's sense of defeat though not
finally willing to participate in it. She, like Gertrude Stein, struggles
for a language in which to make love; that is only one, if not the least,
of my concerns. Now that our sexual experience is increasingly available to us as a subject for contemplation, we have to extend our language to express our new consciousness until we have as many words
for sexuality as the Eskimo has for snow, that pervasive, beautiful,
and mortal climate in which we all live.

Teaching Sexuality

THE FUROR CREATED by the *Body Politic*'s "Men Loving Boys Loving Men" posed hard political questions for me. On the one hand, I deplore repressive police action designed not only to stifle any discussion of the subject of sexual activity across generations but to intimidate anyone even so involved with the paper as to be a subscriber. The subscription lists, correspondence, and other copy were seized as well as the issue of the paper in which the article appeared. On the other hand, I understand the rage against sexual exploitation by men not only of children of both sexes but of women and other men, the pleasures of which the *Body Politic* can sometimes be accused of advertising. I am convinced that censoring serious discussion of unconventional sexual relationships does nothing to protect those who might be exploited. To test, to contest, is the only way to reach forward into understanding areas of human experience vulgarized by either taboo or glorification.

As a society, we are so fearful of sexual initiation that we pretend that, by ignoring it, it will not take place. What we really want is not to know when or how it does. We no longer frighten our children with threats of insanity and death as results of masturbation. It is, instead, clumped with picking one's nose, belching, farting, something not to be done in public, by implication not to be done by nice people at all; but we give our children enough privacy so that the guilty pleasure can be discovered and practiced not only alone but in the company of other unsupervised children. Children caught may be shamed; the more sexually aggressive children ostracized; but it is not, as it used to be, a cause for brutal retribution. Our embarassed liberality on this matter does not extend to encounters between children and adults. Though anyone who spends any time with very young children knows that they are aggressively curious about bodies—

everyone's bodies—apt not only to stick a finger in another's eye or nose but to reach for a nipple or penis, we pretend that these assaults have nothing to do with sex, are only part of the random and *innocent* activity which can be ignored or distracted. The adult who actively participates in sexual instruction of children—whether the nurse who teaches a child masturbation as a sedative or the adult male who complies with a four-year-old's demand, "Show me your penis"—is simply criminal.

Sexual education in this culture, when undertaken at all, unlike any other teaching of bodily function or domestic habit, is presented impersonally in abstract diagrams. Once the breast is unavailable for nourishment and the lap outgrown, sexual pleasure is presented as a far-off and nearly mystical reward for years of asexual (or at least secret) behavior. If defecating and eating were left to the same secrecy and chance, we might face the same problems with basic sanitation and nutrition that we do with sex. When the relatively simple task of teaching table manners takes so many years, why do we assume that sexual manners not only needn't be taught but are a criminal activity between adults and children?

Formal sexual initiations in other cultures may serve as bad examples of what we might teach if given permission: the mutilation of female genitals and the equating of sexual satisfaction and the kill in males. Both these puberty rituals express attitudes toward sexuality in our own culture, and it is no wonder that we can therefore be alarmed at exposing children to adult sexuality. If we viewed sex as a basic appetite normally satisfied and gradually cultivated, we would not need to keep our children isolated and in ignorance for so long, building in them what we have ourselves experienced, intense fear and desire which, so long uninstructed, produce dangerous stupidity. Of course we don't want dangerously stupid adults initiating our children. Fear of that leaves the children to themselves, not out of our conviction that children are, in this matter, the best teachers, but by default. We have so little trust in what we have to teach that we not only abdicate our responsibility but label criminal any adult who might attempt instruction.

There are adults who do sexually exploit, damage, and kill children. It makes no more sense to deal with the question, taking them as the norm, than it would to take rapists as the norm for heterosexual relationships between adults. To say that any sexual activity between adults and children is exploitative because of the superior size and power of the adult is really to acknowledge that overall relationships between adults and children are unequal; and why we feel more concerned over children's sexual dependence than over their physical, emotional, and intellectual dependence says more about us as sexual incompetents than as responsible adults.

Children are at our mercy. They are at each other's mercy as well. It makes about as much sense to leave children's sexual nourishment to their peers as it would to assume that the mud pies they make for each other are an adequate lunch. I use the term *sexual* rather than *sensual* because it seems to me that both our embarrassment about and focus on genitals make us the inept sexual creatures most of us are. A child's need for physical contact is as sexual as our own. It takes as little imagination to know that a child's sexual appetite is different from an adult's as it does to figure out that a newborn baby can't eat an apple or a steak. We don't therefore refuse to feed an infant. If children's sexual independence were as thoughtfully worked toward as their learning to feed themselves, masturbation would become the satisfying accomplishment that it should be. Being able to gratify oneself provides an autonomy that is basic to self-respect and therefore respect for others. Sexual play based on the understanding of pleasure can have associated with it as many small courtesies as eating with other people, as much ritual wonder as the most sacred of games. Just as children gradually learn greater autonomy and responsibility in all other aspects of living, so their development in sexuality should be gradual until they come to the choices of commitment in relationship, parenting, not as sex-starved barbarians willing to barter anything for the experience so long forbidden, infantile, gluttonous, and dangerously stupid, but as warm, sexually intelligent human beings.

Until we have a responsible view of our own sexuality, we will go on shirking our responsibility to our children. We live in so homophobic a society that most adults are terrified of expressing any affection with children of their own sex and even discourage those friendships often most meaningful among children. Mothers can be jealous of, rather than delighting in, their daughters' sexuality, so ambivalent about themselves as women that they don't know what sort of victimization to recommend. Fathers compete with sons, warning them off the lotus land of sexual pleasure when they should be preparing to conquer whatever world has been chosen for them, be it military service or medical school. For every child traumatized by overt and brutal sexual treatment, there are many, many more suffering the damage of ignorance and repression which makes masochistic women and sadistic men the norms of our society. The choice is not really between child rape and chastity into late adolescence. Nor is it between perversion and orthodox heterosexuality. We do have the further option of accepting our own sexuality and therefore that of our children as a complex blessing which we and they must learn neither to exploit nor to deny but to enjoy with sensitivity and intelligence.

Such a change in attitude doesn't come quickly or easily. It will not come at all unless we are willing to address the question seriously and openly. Police who use violence and intimidation to silence such discussion, who see in every adult interested in the sexuality of children a molester and murderer, are themselves victims as well as perpetuators of our sexual sickness. If we discover through reading "Men Loving Boys Loving Men" that we question the motives of the men involved, we must as certainly question our own in letting our children choose such experiments while we pretend we don't. We must also examine the motives of all interaction between adults and children, how much has ever been done "for their own good," how much to reinforce our own values, to give us pleasure, before we are too purely suspicious of anything but disinterested altruism in adults who relate to children. More important than judging the quality of other people's experience and relationships is the exercise of our own memories. Certainly my own initiation came long before I was legally adult. Though a number of males around my age offered to participate, a woman ten years my senior was "responsible," at my invitation and encouragement. The only fault I find with that part of my sexual education was the limit her guilt and fear put on our pleasure, the heterosexual pressure even she felt required to put on me. What she did "for my own good" caused both of us pain. If I were to improve on my own experience now, it would not be to protect children from all adult seduction but to make adults easier to seduce, less burdened with fear or guilt, less defended by hypocrisy. If we accepted sexual behavior between children and adults, we would be far more able to protect our children from abuse and exploitation than we are now. They would be free to tell us, as they can about all kinds of other experience, what is happening to them, have our sympathy and support instead of our mute and mistrustful terror. There are a thousand specific questions, all hard to answer, but we can't begin dealing with them until our basic attitude changes. Children are sexual, and it is up to us to take responsibility for their real education. They have been exploited and betrayed long enough by our silence.

Private Parts and Public Figures

THE RELATIVELY NEW freedom of biographers to discuss the sexual nature and experience of their subjects should be welcomed by anyone seriously interested in the nature of the human creature, for we have been treated to our public persons for too long as if they were like the sexless dolls of our childhood, manikins dressed in period to play their parts only in the public show of politics and the arts. But, as *Body Politic* by its very title suggests, neither genitalia nor sexual acts in themselves can, in isolation, tell us much about the person whose total identity and experience are involved. Biographers, like the rest of us, have been culturally conditioned to think of sexuality as "the private parts" of a life, either beneath concern or of prurient interest. Confronted by the possibility that sexual identity and experience can be a significant, perhaps even integrated, part of a person's life, few biographers seem capable of using such material with the balanced insight that is required.

The difficulties should not be minimized. Evidence has often been destroyed; and even when it exists in diaries and letters, it is material more likely to be distorted than discussions of artistic problems or political decisions, moral and romantic notions as inhibiting as the language itself for the accurate and genuine expression of experience. The compounding difficulty, which should be of greatest concern, is the ignorant bias of biographers, most of whom accept responsibility as accurate researchers of the period, few of whom seriously consider their responsibility to educate themselves in not only the psychological but the social bases of sexuality. Even if one wanted an education of that sort, it would not be easily come by, since those texts which exist are in the majority worse than useless.

All three of the biographies to be reviewed here, *George Sand* by Curtis Cate, *The Lonely Hunter* by Virginia Spencer Carr, and *Amy*

by Jean Gould, are worth reading for anyone interested in Amy Lowell, George Sand, or Carson McCullers, all of whom were gifted
writers. Each of the biographers has been meticulous in the ordinary
requirements of research, Cate and Carr unfortunately giving in to
the temptation of thoroughness to include far more peripheral detail
than is useful or clarifying; but at least they provide good source
books, if not always interesting reading. None of them is equipped
to handle the sexual material involved.

If Curtis Cate had been writing about a man as influential as George
Sand was not only in literature but in politics, it is hard to believe
that he would have devoted the amount of time he has to her private
affairs. This is not an error in itself, since it has been a common fault
of biographers to trivialize the personal relationships of great men, to
consider their sexuality, if at all, as either dalliance or a danger to their
autonomous authority. George Sand's relationships with other people were enormously important to her, but Curtis Cate comes to
them with all the prejudice of a man who assumes that sexual and
maternal love are the center of a woman's life, any woman's life, even
if she happens to be the most prolific and, by her contemporaries,
considered to be the greatest writer of the period. That bias colors all
his interpretations of her relationships; and he is not really able to understand any of them, much less integrate them into a total portrait of
the woman. His condescension and sexual platitudes, coupled with
the physical weight of his book, make it often more inviting to hurl
than to read. Of George Sand's mother's bad temper, he says, for
instance, "She had entered the age of menopause, and lacking a man
to assuage her passionate feelings, she sought an emotional outlet in
tempestuous 'scenes.' " George Sand's mother had real grievance
enough not to need that sort of old husband's tale to explain her anger. Even when he is dealing with male sexuality, his frivolousness is
obvious. Of Alfred de Musset's taste in women, Cate must comment
that he went "from bejeweled marquises to musk-scented sluts." It is
no wonder that a man so gross in his notions about heterosexuality
cannot deal with homosexuality at all.

Nearly all George Sand's intimate relationships were with men, and
with the exception of her husband and a couple of others, they were
men younger than she. Cate makes a great deal of George Sand's

masculine qualities at the same time that he works to explain them away. Her masculine dress was more practical for riding in the country, the only costume that would let her into the pit for cheap tickets to the theatre when she was running short of money. And, though he gives room to such descriptions of her as Alfred de Vigny's "A man in turn of phrase, language, sound of voice, and boldness of expression," he restricts these qualities to her writing self and always interprets her relationships with men as either childish or maternal. "At twenty [George Sand] was still erotically underdeveloped," and it must have hurt her husband's "masculine pride to realize that he could not overcome his wife's basic frigidity." As a more mature woman, she restricted her lovers sexually because, according to Cate, in a motherly way she feared for their health. Chopin was consumptive, and apparently, except in the early stages of their relationship, George Sand insisted on abstinence. A lover after Chopin also developed consumption. Cate does not speculate that George Sand in her maturity may have been drawn to men who precisely wouldn't make great sexual demands on her.

Cate insists that the gossip about George Sand as a lesbian, though abundant, was simply malicious. In any case, for all the men she was involved with, there was only one woman who importantly attracted her: Marie Dorval, an actress. In the intense beginning of their relationship, Marie Dorval often went from the theatre to George Sand and spent the night, a habit explained by Cate as simply one of convenience, since Alfred de Vigny, Marie's lover, would be asleep at that hour, and George Sand was accustomed to staying up through the night. He does not go on to deal with the fact that, except with Marie Dorval, George Sand reserved those hours exclusively for her writing. "That the tête-à-tête occasionally become [sic] a corps-à-corps is possible though I personally doubt it." He doubts it *because* George Sand was "obsessed by the idea that she was too masculine . . . " And he goes on to say that, therefore, she "must in any case have been a gauche and timid lover." It seems, quite to the contrary, that she pressed her affair with Marie Dorval so urgently it finally caused a break between them. Alfred de Vigny wrote across a plaintive letter George Sand sent to Marie, "I've forbidden Marie to reply to this Sappho who bores her."

At pains to prove she was not a lesbian, Cate also wants to be sure he does not give the impression she might have been sympathetic to women's liberation today, for, though she took a strong stand against marriage, she was not in favor of granting women the vote. George Sand, in these dangerous times, must not be made a model for contemporary woman but must be retained in the role of maternal lover, indulgent and protective. The fact that her reputation as a writer has suffered since her time makes it the easier to focus on her as a woman who, though dedicated to democratic principles and an advocate of them, refused as ludicrous the suggestion that she run for office.

The point is not that George Sand was a lesbian or a women's libber. Her life has been taken into the hands of a biographer who wants to dominate her as no man in her life had been able to. Necrophilia is hardly the most clarifying sexual stance for a biographer.

If the abundance of detail in *George Sand* works to bully its subject, the same failing in *The Lonely Hunter* tends to trivialize Carson McCullers. Virginia Spencer Carr does not lack sympathy for her subject. She is far more dedicated than, I suspect, most readers can be to a writer of great gifts who seems to have had very few as a human being. Egotistical, emotionally dependent, physically frail, Carson McCullers was a clinging tyrant in her relationships with other people. Elizabeth Bowen, who endured her twice as a house guest, said, "I always felt Carson was a destroyer; for which reason I chose never to be closely involved with her." Reeves, her weak and abused and abusive husband, contemplated killing her and finally killed himself. Only Tennessee Williams seems to have lasted the course of her life, faithful in his indulgence of and admiration for her. It was a life with enough melodramatic urgency, crisis, and catastrophe to have made a fairly hair-raising, at times hilarious, at times tragic story; and some of the other players, like W. H. Auden, Gypsy Rose Lee, and Katharine Anne Porter, are colorful enough in themselves to present challenging technical problems to keep them in their minor roles. Carr, however, continually interrupts the thrust of that life with domestic trivia, medical speculation, truly minor characters who have value only for the interviews they granted her, and finally tentative explanations of Carson McCullers designed, for the most part, to keep her from entirely exasperating her reading audience as she did most of her live audience with drunken antics, not very good piano recitals, and cries for help. That Carson McCullers could produce the amount of work she did against the pressure of both real and imagined illness, finally crippling strokes, is due to her own remarkable dedication as an artist and to the uncritical and unwavering support offered to her by her mother and later by Mary Mercer, a doctor who attended her in the last bedridden years of her life.

Carr's attempts to deal with Carson McCullers's sexual nature and involvements are neither so obtuse nor so defensive as Cate's with George Sand. She is more often descriptive than analytical, and she doesn't fall into the obvious psychoanalytic traps that make McCullers's life often look like a Freudian mine field. Though Carr does spend a good deal of time examining the relationship Carson had with her mother, who proclaimed her daughter's genius at birth, frankly favored her above the other children, and tended her in illness as if it were not simply the first but the only requirement of her life, Carr does not automatically associate this dependency with Carson's passions for women all through her life. Carr's attempt is to make that range of Carson's sexual nature simply a fact. "Not to be interested in sex with men . . . was as much a part of her physiological make-up as having two legs, arms, a heart, and a brain." But, if that is so, why does Carr also say of Reeves, "he was incapable of coping with his wife's sexual inclinations or of helping her to become more heterosexually oriented"?

The passions Carson McCullers conceived for people as diverse as Greta Garbo and Katherine Anne Porter, her presentation of herself as a young genius worthy to worship at their feet (she literally threw herself at the feet of Katherine Anne Porter, who stepped over her in order not to be late to dinner) were consistently rebuffed; but her involvement with Erika Mann and through her with Annemarie Clarac-Schwarzenbach was of a different order, since with these two women she hoped for an all-embracing rapport, and perhaps she came closer to it with Annemarie than with anyone else. Her desire to be lover rather than beloved, her belief that the roles could not be reciprocal, were sources of insight in her work but made her own life ludicrous and painful much of the time. It isn't bisexuality, as Carr tentatively suggests, which was at the root of Carson's unhappy relationships with people, but a preoccupation with herself, compounded by the requirements of artistic dedication and severe illness. But at least this biographer doesn't make an authority of her ignorance, and it is better for Carson McCullers to suffer at the hands of sympathy and a profusion of not clearly structured details than at the hands of a misinformed expert or bigot.

Jean Gould is sorry that Ada Dwyer Russell, the woman Amy Lowell lived with for many years, did not write anything about their relationship to contribute understanding "especially to those troubled with a psychosexual conflict such as Amy Lowell's." Without that testimony Gould dabbles in a number of popular theories. She claims a "dominance of masculine genes in Amy," who as a child was "seemingly as much a boy as a girl, as if she had literally sprung from her father's loins." It is typical of her style to offer first a bit of unsubstantiated medical lore and then to add mythological reference so that Amy Lowell is never in danger of being presented as a case history but always as larger-than-life as she was. But, as if uncertain that the genetic theory is sound enough, Gould also explains Amy's being a tomboy as the result of her having no companions her own age and imitating her brothers and father because she admired them. The balance for this earnest analysis is a comic story about Amy's signing a letter to her parents, "Your loving son, Amy," because she couldn't spell *daughter*.

Amy Lowell's gross overweight, even in adolescence, contributed to her own sense of herself as "a great, rough, masculine, strong thing," but it did not make her envious or shy of other girls her age. "She seemed to gravitate toward the prettiest girls in school." In her diary, she acknowledged the kind of relationship she wanted: "I feel very much in need of a *very* intimate friend, a friend whom I should love better than any other girl in the world & who would feel so toward me . . . we should love to be alone together, both of us." The reciprocity Amy Lowell required and obviously achieved in her relationship with Ada Russell was part of her larger pride in her identity as a Lowell, one of the great and wealthy eastern families, and in herself as a poet. The early attempts of her mother to force her into a more conventional mode, refusing to let her act a male role in a play, making an effort to see her properly married, were only temporary distractions from the character she would develop. There were rumors of a fiancé who left town, the explanation for a trip abroad and a session of severe dieting which left Amy Lowell in a deep lassitude for a long time. The biographer, while admitting that some were convinced there never was a fiancé, makes much of Amy Lowell's suffering from unrequited heterosexual love, not only in this experience but later, in her long friendship with Carl Engel, as if these, too, could explain her final sexual choices.

If Amy Lowell had wanted a husband, she could have purchased one not only with her actual wealth but with her position. She might have been too proud for such a solution, but she would also have been at a loss to know what to do with one, for, as she herself explained, "I cannot help admiring, and generally falling in love with, extreme beauty." After seeing Duse, the famous actress, perform in Boston, Amy Lowell, "with masculine aggression, followed her idol to Philadelphia." She later courted Ada, also an actress, with the same energy.

Always attracted to the theater, Amy Lowell was a real actress herself. She loved to produce plays at her own house, and she thoroughly enjoyed the reading and lecturing tours once she was an established poet. She liked to "play" herself, a large, forthright woman who smoked cigars, part of that pleasure being that to unwrap a cigar was like "undressing a lady." And she carried herself into her business dealings with publishers and editors in the same way, assured, hardheaded, proud.

Amy Lowell and Gertrude Stein were almost exact contemporaries, and Gould compares them, claiming that they both contributed "by the lives they led, to the liberation of women, lesbian or otherwise, the world over." The difficulty with this claim is that the life Amy Lowell and Gertrude Stein both led was based on social privilege. Neither was dependent on social approval for survival. Amy Lowell had even less political consciousness than Gertrude Stein. Only at the end of her life did Amy Lowell develop paranoia about those classes of people suffering poor working conditions and wages in the mills owned by her family, and then her concern was not for them but for herself. Liberation for Amy Lowell was entirely a personal matter.

Sex roles are very much linked with power, and a great many of

Amy Lowell's mannerisms and tastes which are offered as secondary sex characteristics indicative of her sexual needs may have been much more importantly related to her desire for power, not necessarily in a sexual relationship at all, but in the world where she fought to be recognized, not just as the sister of the president of Harvard University, not just as a Lowell, but as herself, an accomplished poet. One of her ambitions was to have the president of Harvard known more importantly as "the brother of Amy Lowell." In her relationship with Ada, though she may have wanted to assert her authority, there are indications that it was a far more equal partnership, because Ada insisted on a businesslike salary for her part in organizing Amy Lowell's life and on freedom to visit with her family and friends as she chose. Amy's nickname for Ada was Peter, as if it were important to lift her, too, into an identity of privilege.

As a biography, *Amy* is the most ambitious in attempting to bring private and public person into focus together. Though Gould can introduce some conventional regrets for Amy Lowell's failure in heterosexual love, she happily acknowledges that Ada was the source of Amy Lowell's greatest poems. "If her impetus toward heterosexual love had not been checked—to her tragic disappointment at the time—she might never have been more than a Boston clubwoman and society matron running a semi-literary salon." Gould ends the biography by quoting Amy Lowell's "In Excelsis," whose mood is evident in just a fragment:

> So you- air- earth- heaven-
> I do not thank you,
> I take you
> and live.

Perhaps what these biographers all fail to do is to deal with the reciprocal pressures of sexuality and society, the part money and privilege or lack of it plays in sexual choice, how little "masculine" and "feminine" traits have to do with sex at all but with power or lack of it. At least both Jean Gould and Virginia Carr respect the sexual experience of their subjects, though they may not always understand it. Curtis Cate, for all his asserting to the contrary, has not been able to reduce George Sand to his own needs; and though this is, by far, the worst biography of the three, George Sand remains the most politically perceptive because she understood the relationship between private and public lives, even if her own was imperfectly related to her knowledge.

We do not want or need biographers who come to the lives of their subjects with a tidy sexual or political theory for analysis and judgment. What is required is the knowledge that, if sexuality is a legitimate subject for the biographer, the clichés of the culture are not sufficient for dealing with it. Explaining or explaining away sexual identity and experience are not the point. Restoring human beings to their wholeness in our perception of them is the job of biographer and citizen alike. As long as who and what we desire are treated as broken-off secrets of our lives, trivial for men, all-consuming for women, we will go on understanding very little about what it is to be human, in public or private.

With All Due Respect

SEVERAL YEARS AGO I volunteered to set up a seminar called "Lesbian Life Styles" as one of a number of offerings for a large, noncredit women's studies course at the University of British Columbia. I did not limit enrollment because it did not occur to me that very many women would feel free to attend. On the first night forty women registered, and through the twelve weeks the seminar met there was a floating population of well over fifty. Those with some experience in the women's movement wanted an open discussion without a chairperson; and though the group was obviously too large for many of the women to feel free to speak, no one was willing to break up into smaller groups, at first perhaps because of the pleasure of being in a room with so many women willing to call themselves lesbians, but quite soon out of fear of being isolated in smaller and more vulnerable numbers. For that room (it was my own living room) had become a very dangerous place to be, heavy with mistrustful silences, defensiveness, and hostility. Having been asked not to direct the group in any way, not to sit in my "Archie Bunker" chair (yes, I'm afraid I do have one, and it even looks very like my father's chair where we used to fish in the cracks for loose change to go to the movies), I waited out the first few weeks with hopeful patience, telling myself that we probably just had to get through a period of testing to a time when people would be willing to move into smaller groups and speak with the open candor I had come to associate with other women's meetings. But the atmosphere didn't improve; it deteriorated. I could not understand why people came back week after week. If the meetings had not been at my house, I would have given up in a month.

There were plenty of explanations for what happened. The age range was from eighteen to fifty-five; occupations were as diverse as laundry worker and professor of psychology. There were Maoists and devout Catholics. Some were members of a commune. There were monogamous couples, married women living with their husbands and female lovers, single parents who hid their lovers or explained their lovers to their children, women who had never dared approach the women they loved for fear of rejection. Such diversity doesn't need to get in the way of sharing experiences, but in this circumstance it did. One by one every woman who was willing to speak was disqualified by others in the room as inauthentic, not a "real" lesbian. Women without sexual experience were rejected; women who associated with men were rejected; monogamous couples did not have the political consciousness to be lesbians; political lesbians were only using the label as a gimmick. Night after night people did nothing but defend their own right to be lesbian and discredit others whose notions were different from their own. A great many people never spoke at all.

Finally, with only two meetings left I couldn't stand it any longer. I sat down in my Archie Bunker chair and made my reactionary speech. It was *my* house, and I was left every week to clean up the psychic blood that had been spilled. If people wanted to go on with the destruction, I'd get them a room at the university for the last two meetings. If people came back to the house again, I would assert my right to chair the meeting if people still refused to meet in smaller groups, to dictate topics, to cut off hostile speeches. Some people decided to meet elsewhere. Some came back. The day after the last meeting a couple of young women appeared at my door with a single rose, saying, "We met and fell in love in your seminar; so it couldn't have been all bad."

I don't even now know how much the atmosphere of those meetings was my inadvertent doing, my assumption of a basic goodwill among people which simply didn't exist, nor do I know how much of the hostility people directed at each other might really have been meant for me, but I did feel a heavy responsibility for the damage done to so many people who, given their circumstances, could ill afford attacks by those from whom they might expect support. My frank disapproval of what was going on only added another flavor of bitterness to the experience.

To be a public lesbian, to dare to wear the label even in a group like that or perhaps particularly in a group like that—is to insist that the psychic and moral content of the word be changed, its connotations made positive rather than negative. But what is positive to one lesbian is negative to another, and differing values become at once conflicting values. For, if one woman asserts her right to wear boots and a jeans jacket as an image of her freedom to be who she is, another who wants people to understand that "lesbians are just like anybody else" feels profoundly threatened. If one woman is trying to work out a loving and open relationship with both her husband and the woman she loves, another with a partner who is tempted by the safety of a heterosexual marriage feels betrayed and morally outraged. The lesbian who is willing to sacrifice everything for the privilege of being public in every circumstance, who sees any other choice as cowardly, confronts the lesbian mother with the loss of her children, the schoolteacher or nurse with the loss of her job.

The conflicts that I saw in my living room are also being played out in the larger public world. Robin Morgan discredits Jill Johnston for being politically incorrect. Others discredit Robin Morgan because she is married and has a child. And Kate Millett can't figure out, moving from community to community, whether she's supposed to call herself bisexual or lesbian, because what is momentarily all right on the east coast turns out to be wrong on the west coast. There is not, apparently, an authentic lesbian in the land, except perhaps those who have yet to admit it. To discover this at a time when thousands of women are choosing to take the risk of being public lesbians is at first disconcerting and then for many really terrifying. It ought, I think sadly, to be funny.

For those of us who were public lesbians long before there was a movement which seemed to promise support, the rule-making, the testing and the infighting are not as threatening as for those women who have counted on some sympathy and protection in order to take the risk in the first place. I don't mean to suggest that we pre-movement lesbians are either wiser or more courageous. The choice for many was forced upon us and had to be dealt with more like a broken leg than a heroic stance. For others the choice had more practical advantages than disadvantages, providing a defense against marriage or relief from burdensome family relationships or a way out of work we didn't like in the first place. Even those few who were actually crusaders usually enlisted in the battle under pen names when writing for magazines like *The Ladder*. When we met other lesbians, we did not automatically assume sympathy. On the contrary, we accepted the danger of increased visibility and usually avoided each other except at carefully arranged private meetings. "Don't worry about dress," I was told by a lesbian in her sixties who was inviting me to Sunday lunch, "we'll be just queers." We all knew people who had lost jobs and children just by having been seen with one of us. We learned to be negatively protective. There was no illusion that, when we walked in the bright light of day, we would have the support or even the approval of our sisters. What we did learn was to live without it, to come to terms with our own lives without the aid or the threat of the group. It's not an easy lesson, and it leaves some people in places of fear and bitterness who know, when they see what is happening among lesbians now, that people are really no damned good, and the only solution is to go on marching through life fully armed. (We grew up on Steig cartoons.) But for others of us the movement really has provided some real support, new choices, and new friends; and since we aren't as badly shaken by disapproval and rejection, having learned to live with it, perhaps we have a special job in the movement to work against what divides us and for a kind of solidarity that is real.

Six months ago, against the protests of my nervous system, I set up another seminar, because I was working on a book called *Lesbian Images*, chiefly made up of literary and biographical studies of writers like Gertrude Stein, Willa Cather, Radclyffe Hall, Vita Sackville-West, Margaret Anderson, etcetera, and I wanted some feedback from other lesbians. The group was much smaller; and though real differences existed, everyone there shared an interest in books. The questions raised too personally in the first seminar could be dealt with at one remove when they were found in books. Why were so many of these writers involved with masculine identities? If they were influenced by the economic and political circumstances of their time and place, why was someone like Margaret Anderson apparently completely free of defining her relationships in masculine and feminine terms? Maureen Duffy, the youngest of the writers I was considering, born in England in 1933 into the working class, was nearly as rigid as Radclyffe Hall in asserting masculine identity, drawing heavily on Freud. We could discuss the influences of various psychological theories on these writers, the effect religious faith had on some of them. Radclyffe Hall, for instance, was a devout Catholic. Did class influence their sexual attitudes? Vita Sackville-West was an aristocrat; Gertrude Stein worshipped the values of the solid middle class; Maureen Duffy grew up in the slums of southern England. There were very few personal comments in those discussions; but often after a seminar, individual members of it would tell me of long conversations with their friends and lovers afterwards, sometimes amiable, sometimes intense and defensive. "May Sarton is going to ruin my life," one of them announced. "The woman I live with is absolutely taken with Sarton's notion that you need a new muse for each new book."

Among the writers themselves and the characters in their books, people found concepts and experiences similar to their own, threatening to their own, simply puzzling. "Why was Violette Leduc such a victim with men? Why did she fall in love with male homosexuals?" "Maybe to make it impossible, so that she kept time for herself." While we read and discussed, we were becoming more aware of the great diversity of experience in our until recently neglected and hidden heritage, which has always had its advocates of monogamy, bisexuality, celibacy, communal living, and motherhood, which has always struggled with questions about psychology, religion, and class. But it was also clear that, if we were to understand these women, we had to know them not only as advocates but as individual people limited and strengthened by their particular experiences and capacities. "Margaret Anderson was a silly woman in some ways, but I can't help liking her for the delight she took in living." We were finding not models for living but companions and friends, an experience which made us more companionable and friendly with each other, not unaware of our real differences but able to let them exist without constant defensiveness.

Support is a much used word in the women's movement. For too many people it means giving and receiving unqualified approval.

Some women are awfully good at feigning that for long periods of time and just as good at withdrawing it at crucial moments. Too many are convinced that they can't function without it. It's a false concept which has produced barriers to understanding and done real emotional damage. Suspension of critical judgment is not necessary for offering real support, which has to do instead with self-respect and respect for other people even at moments of serious disagreement. I have been critical of Jill Johnston's pressuring of other people to be as public as she is, not because it threatens me, for I stand very much with her in public, but because I don't believe total visibility would necessarily achieve the better world she believes in. I have been critical of the amount of fear and hostility Robin Morgan has found it necessary to express because I think those emotions are contagious. I don't like Kate Millett's occasional flirtation with the role of public victim chiefly because I care about Kate Millett. I do, however, respect the right of each of those women to choose what she chooses; and given the privilege of arguing with any one of them, I would contend as I do with a lover, to know and be known, without will to discredit, without will to win or lose, in a contest designed to strengthen both people. That attitude is possible only when I first of all accept that none of these women ever speaks for me, any more than Gertrude Stein or Radclyffe Hall or Vita Sackville-West speaks for me. I speak for myself. We must all finally speak for ourselves. I don't mean each of us should be able to command large audiences. Frankly, the dangers of serving a large audience often outweigh the values, for too many women are tempted to think of people like Robin and Kate and Jill as "leaders," therefore required to represent all women, though none of them has ever stood for election. They are self-appointed only as we are all self-appointed to speak our own minds. Each of us is, in that sense, alone; and if there is terror in that knowledge, there is also relief. No one else can discredit my life if it is in my own hands, and therefore I do not have to make anyone else carry the false burden of my frightened hostility. The paradox is that, when I really stand alone, I realize what remarkably good and large company I am in. There are authentic lesbians everywhere: yes, asleep in their husbands' arms; yes, nursing their children; yes, three to a bed; yes, faithful into old age; yes, alone. Each has to stand alone before we can walk together, even in twos and threes, never mind as an army of lovers.

Homophobia and Romantic Love

"Do you mean there are lesbians *here*, in this room?" a young woman asked, horrified. For her the experience of women meeting together once a week, sometimes as many as fifty of them, to break up into small groups and discuss the problems shared by women, had been literally liberating from the sexual pressure she always felt when men were around. That she might have to be on her sexual guard again, this time with women, depressed her badly. A man, reviewing Kate Millett's *Sita* in the *New York Times*, confessed to a depression (the sincerity of which I doubt) because *even* in a lesbian relationship one woman dominated the other emotionally and, more blatantly, sexually. If lesbian sexuality poses all the same problems, while being "a problem" in itself, it is automatically worse. The onus is on the lesbian to prove to heterosexual women and men that her experience is essentially better, if it is to be accepted at all. There is a lot of attractive arrogance, particularly among younger lesbians setting out to do just that, and they have my candid applause for every point they win in the debate. Having grown up in the lesbian silence of the 30s and 40s, having had no sense of community through the 50s, having broken the silence for myself in the early 60s with a gentle and romantic novel, I have developed no skills for that debate, but Adrienne Rich's invitation to enter into a conversation about homophobia in all women, not necessarily in political/feminist terms, but to discover "what's really going on here," calls to my own endless wondering at experience.

If I had been the same age as the young woman who was threatened by the idea of lesbians in the same room, I would perhaps have been angry with her, though when I was her age and a friend of mine expressed the same kind of horror ("What would you do if you ever met a lesbian? I think I'd throw up or faint or die.") I said not a word; and later, in my brooding, neither anger nor any doubt about my silence ever crossed my mind. I felt simply horribly and inevitably alone. Twenty-five years later, I wanted to be instructive, and I think I was gentle and reassuring enough to encourage that young woman to be courteous if not open-minded about experience. I suspect my own sexuality, because of my age and my position as a university teacher, was unreal to her, as I am sure the sexuality of her male teachers even older than I was not. I could not, in good faith, have told her that no lesbian would ever find her attractive and make sexual advances. Most in my generation are timid and circumspect enough to be generally harmless, but lesbians her own age might certainly not only desire her but feel some political zeal in converting her, challenge and bully with as much ego investment as any young male for conquest. Nor, of course, could I have assured any young lesbian that one of her adventuresome heterosexual sisters might not take advantage of her feelings for the experience of it. The young call it "doing numbers" on each other.

I *am* sincerely depressed by how often lesbian relationships are accurate caricatures of heterosexual relationships, though it doesn't surprise me. It's important for Kate Millett to chart accurately what has happened to her, whether anyone is depressed by it or not. It is clear that Kate's obsession with Sita depends on Sita's indifference at this stage in the relationship. The moment Sita relents, offers Kate the sexual security and attention she craves, Kate feels claustrophobic and longs to be free. Over and over again I was reminded of Willa Cather's statement: "Human relationships are the tragic necessity of human life; that they can never be wholly satisfactory, that every ego is half the time greedily seeking them, and half the time pulling away from them."

True. For my much younger self. I was sexually so hungry, humanly so isolated, psychically so traumatized by social judgment that I required of myself a purity of motive so self-sacrificing, a vision of love so redeeming that to be a lover was an annihilation of all the healthy instincts of self-preservation I had. I am still not free of all the phobic reactions that sweet, strong, young self had to resort to in order to stay singularly alive. And though we say over and over again that the young now are not traumatized as we were, I do not really believe that the sexual revolution of the women's movement has reached most nervous systems yet. I was interrupted in the middle of this paragraph by a phone call from a younger friend who said, "My lover, ever since a political fight about tenure at her university eighteen months ago, has vomited every time we have made love, which has been no more than once every two months, and now she's moved into the guest room and says I should make love to anyone else I want." There's the homophobia in ourselves, Adrienne, whether we've known from age eight or only discovered after years of marriage and childbearing that we love each other. No wonder the homophobia in heterosexual men and women is so outrageous to us. Before we confront it in them, never mind that's where we got it, we must understand it in ourselves.

As honestly as I can recall, before I knew any psychological or moral definitions, I turned to women for love because I knew how I wanted to be loved, and I knew only women knew that. From my mother certainly. I had a cherishing father when he was around, but he was rarely around, and so he loved ideas he had made of his children. My mother loved us through our vomitings, broken bones, sulks; listened to our jokes, theories about the world, egomanias, and sorrows. (My father, this day, loves as I think a woman can, but it has taken him seventy-odd years to come to it, and he's rarely gifted.) I did not think then about being loved, though I needed to be. I thought about being loving.

I was not good at it, "half the time greedily seeking . . . half the time pulling away . . . " I could not get clear of the separation of roles, beloved or lover. Like Kate and Sita, I seesawed between senses of power and dependence. Power required too much responsibility. Dependence was too humiliating. In each is the failure to be peer, a failure that is so appalling in the heterosexual model, never mind that some men and women together figure out how to be free of it.

Do we begin by disliking ourselves as women because women are unequally loved? Do we carry that dislike into our love of other women and therefore struggle under a burden: knowing we are worse, we must, therefore, be better? Are we the unclean bitches who must transform ourselves into goddesses? To try to be too good to be true is spiritually so expensive that our failures not only nauseate but destroy numbers of us. I wrote some years ago, "I'd like to try being simply good enough."

It was my lovers who suffered nauseous guilt, not I. They returned to husbands, the church, celibate scholarship. I, instead, found I could not walk down a city street, stand before an audience, eat in front of anyone. I slept, drank, masturbated through days to avoid writing and believed my will to defy those escapes and get back to work would finally kill me. It is not simply a story of the terrible 50s. I hear it all around me now in the "liberated" 70s.

I understand why Bertha Harris wants to insist that lesbians, the only true lesbians, are monsters. She is trying to take our homophobia into her arms and transform herself/us into lovers "bad enough to be true," incestuous, self-centered, addicted, mad. Begin to love there.

I lack the romantic flair, live in too small a community (by choice), have been too long in a central relationship (twenty-three years, by choice). I need more ordinary solutions. Or hopes.

One of my heterosexual friends told me that her lover had said she wasn't a good "wife" to him. She asked him for his definition of a wife. When he had finished telling her, she said, "You're not talking about a wife; you're talking about the mother of a child under six." I am always nervous about the suggestion that, as lesbians, we should mother each other, though I understand that the image comes from our first source of love. Our mothers are also the first source of rejecting power against whom we screamed our dependent rage. As adults, if we cry out for that mother love, the dependent rage inevitably follows, and what is even more disconcerting is that, given total attention and sympathy, we are soon restless to be free, for we aren't any longer children. A young man asked me, in a seminar on Willa Cather, "Don't you think only people of the same sex can have a *real* marriage, not only of the flesh but of the imagination?" "I don't know," I answered, "but what a dreadful thought!" "One flesh" has always struck me as spurious, since each is importantly defined by a sack of skin, and children are not metaphors of union but individuals often made up of gene banks hard to recognize as in any way similar to either parent. "One imagination" is an even more terrifying invasion of the autonomous mind and spirit.

The Greeks treated romantic passion like any other illness, expressed sympathy and a hope for early recovery. Yet we put the state of being in love as the highest good. When I encounter people "entirely in love," I wonder why we couldn't just as well celebrate any delirious fever, say pneumonia, as a state infinitely to be desired. Surely we would be kinder to ourselves and our friends to hope for a cure than to encourage a lifelong ailment, fortunately very rare.

I am not being cynical. The love which Kate Millett describes in *Sita* is finally degrading to both people, patterned as it is on the relationship between a mother and a dependent child. Kate's instinct to get out, to get back to her own work, is her cure. Both the pain of her own dependence and Sita's return to men as lovers strengthen the homophobia in each of them. There can be no lasting delight and nourishment between people when one is always afraid the other will return to "Daddy" with his superior sexual power, the other sure to be suffocated by a possessive child who refuses to grow up and leave home.

I don't think there is any way to root out our homophobia until we also deal with the infantile in romantic love as the weed that it is, choking out the young and real sisterhood that begins to flower among us. We have got to be peers, respecting each other's strengths without dependent envy, sympathetic with each other's weaknesses without cherishing or encouraging them, interdependent by choice, not by terrified necessity.

I love the eroticism among women who like their own bodies, the hard discussion between those who require their own minds, the joy among strong spirits. The young woman who was terrified to be in a room with lesbians learned her fear from men who tried to dominate her. The man depressed at the old pattern of sexual politics, even between two women, was first disillusioned about relationship in heterosexual terms. Each is projecting onto lesbians the basic failure of romantic love between the sexes. If we try to be better at that, we will over and over again feel worse.

Sex is not so much an identity as a language which we have for so long been forbidden to speak that most of us learn only the crudest of its vocabulary and grammar. If we are to get past the pattern of dominance and submission, of possessive greed, we must outgrow love as fever, as "the tragic necessity of human life," and speak in tongues that set us free to be loving equals.

Stumps

IT IS SAID of the community I live in that we don't cooperate for anything short of a forest fire. This is an exaggeration. We have not only a volunteer fire department but a community hall and a park we supervise ourselves. However, any newly proposed community responsibility elicits no more than indifference or bickering. Most people have stayed or come here because of an appetite for solitude to avoid the interference government is allowed in larger communities, the allegiance required by groups with similar beliefs and aims. When we talk, we expect to disagree. All communities are, in fact, enemy territory for the individual, even those which profess concern for consensus, because none can accommodate comfortably all that anyone is. This community doesn't try.

It is in just this climate, a microcosm of indifference, misunderstanding, and mistrust, I like to learn how to live. When the CBC tried to do a program suggesting that we are turning into an artists' colony, everyone scoffed, including the people interviewed. Because there are a number of independent women here, rumor in the San Francisco bars has it that this island is about to be renamed Lesbos. If I ever did find myself in an artists' colony or lesbian community, I'd move.

Once I wanted very much to belong. Moving from place to place where I was always the stranger, object of suspicion and scorn, I dreamed of being with friends I had known all my life not just for security but for the positive pleasure of shared experiences, shared attitudes. Once I stayed in a town long enough to go back to school a second year, and there in the classroom was a new student, fat, nearly blind, and terrified. I was allowed to join the rest of the class in chasing her across the playground, down the steps, and into the street. I threw one of her galoshes after her. Alone on my way home, I threw

up my lunch and my breakfast. I have never since met solidarity
that didn't sooner or later have to do with throwing galoshes or
worse, and my stomach for it is no stronger than it was when I was ten.
Lack of solidarity here is our greatest virtue. We are good citizens
to the extent that we agree to disagree with only an occasional flare of
righteous indignation at an NDP* billboard in front of someone's
house, a women's liberation sticker on one of the Easter eggs at the
hunt, a Jesus Christ Superstar button, an Anita Bryant bumper sticker,
all of which are the signs of our diversity. I stay fairly visible not only
because my books are exchanged at the monthly fire hall book sale,
not only because I occasionally say my piece on the CBC, but because I refer to myself as a lesbian in ordinary conversation at the post
office or on the dock. My young nieces come here for the summer,
my parents for their fiftieth wedding anniversary. Friends arrive who
are black, oriental, in nun's robes, in blue jeans, on crutches, with gui-
tars, bicycles, kites, portfolios, in Landrovers and Lincolns. They do
not look like, nor are they, an army. They are known and watched
as I am to see what there is to fear. The only fantasy I have about a
takeover of this island is by the trees; there are enough loggers to prevent that. They are visible, too.

"The forest is our garden," they say. "Trees are weeds."

Elisabeth Hopkins, who lives just up the road, has given me a water-
color of a stump. On my study door is a copy of the Emily Carr
"Scorned as Timber, Beloved of Sky" trees, tall, spindly, and light-
struck standing singly in the wreckage of a lumbering off. In the
scrub forest I see the branches of a fallen tree begin to behave like
trees themselves, growing upward. I write in my notebook, "I should
write a novel called *Stumps.*"

"Writers?" the real estate agent says to an interviewer. "Sure, they
come over here on Canada Council Grants to write dirty books."

We all resent each other's use of the raw material. But nobody in
this kind of small community can trust the prejudice of enough other
people to act. We are an environment in political balance, each with
enough natural enemies to keep our numbers down if we are to stay
adequately nourished. In such a place it is easiest to learn both the
danger and necessity of visibility. It is as clear what it would cost
island economy to kill me as to kill a logger, real estate agent, fisher-

man, schoolteacher. Human beings tolerate what they understand they have to tolerate. Only visibility is instruction. One of my neighbors said to another, after reading *Lesbian Images*, "I'd rather not know; but as long as she doesn't try to convert me, it's her business how she lives."

In a city that "would rather not know," visibility is a harder business. The police enjoy protecting that ignorance, bolstering prejudice in raids on everything from steam baths to newspapers, providing lurid copy. People begin to think they don't have to tolerate that. Nothing as simple as a parade will change their minds. Only when a community knows that everywhere in all circumstances it is shared by gay people does it learn, as San Francisco has, that it must accept us as part of the political reality. If we stay invisible or withdraw into protective communities, we are dangerously disturbing the political balance on which we need to depend.

Here on this cranky little island, the lesson is clear. No matter how much we may quarrel about how to live, no matter how grudgingly we accept each other's company, no matter what conflicting uses we put our forests to, we know we don't want to burn it down. We have only ourselves to depend on, and everyone is needed. Lightning, a tourist, a defective woodstove, could still defeat us and may, but we do have some protection from the destructiveness in ourselves, because we live without police or parades with a great deal we'd rather not know and have to know in order to survive.

---

* New Democratic Party (Canada)

Letters

I SAVE THE letters written to me about my work. From the time my first novel, *Desert of the Heart*, came out in 1964, there have been many more than I expected, thanking, asking for help, challenging, telling their own stories. A writer for some people is like the stranger on a plane, someone to confide in, with a real, if only half-consciously recognized, difference: the stranger is chosen as someone unlikely to betray secrets; the writer, on the other hand, is a teller of tales. Though some of my correspondents have offered their life stories as material for books I ought to write, I have never used material from any of the letters. Yet I feel my heart far better informed for them, the range of my understanding greater. And they, as much as if not more than reviews, describe the climate in which my books have been written.

For their sociological and psychological value, archivists have argued that the letters should be among the papers preserved for the library. When that suggestion was first made, I protested that people who write to me don't imagine that their sometimes very personal revelations will end up in the public archives. Though I didn't write books for the purpose of soliciting people's confidings, once I received them I felt I had a trust, protecting the real people who wrote those letters from exposure and abuse. To that objection, a fifty-year seal was suggested. In, let us say, the year 2030, there would be no one left with any personal stake in the letters, and their social value could be fairly assessed. Though the dead can't be legally libeled, I feel no freer to abuse their memory. Yet, I wondered, isn't one of the motives in writing to become part of the testimony of what it has been like to be alive? To destroy the letters might be a greater offense than to save them.

I talked with a number of people who argued on both sides. For some, privacy is absolute. To expose it no matter how far into the future is a betrayal. I have friends whose letters, at their request, I routinely destroy once I've answered them. Others, however, feel just as strongly that our personal lives belong to history, and to destroy evidence is to participate in the lie that reduces the truth to a guilty secret.

One afternoon when an archivist was visiting and helping me to sort out various other problems about preserving papers, I told her that I hadn't been able yet to make a decision about the letters. She was still arguing strongly for their inclusion in the archives.

"Would you mind if I looked at some of them?" she asked.

Though for some clear-eyed moralists this request in itself would be a violation of privacy, I felt no hesitation, respecting as I do this woman's discretion. I thought if she could see the range of the material she might understand better both my hesitation and my concern. I handed her the file of letters written after *Lesbian Images* came out, then offered her a cup of tea or a drink, which she refused. I went off upstairs to get myself something and also to start dinner. By the time I got back down to my study, she was sitting with the file in her lap, staring at the fire.

"Could I change my mind about that drink?"

"Of course," I said and went to get her one.

When I got back, she asked for a cigarette as well. She doesn't ordinarily smoke.

After some moments of silence, she said, "These should be burned, all of them, right now."

"You begin to see the problems they pose for me?"

"One of them," she said, "is from a good friend of mine."

I stood, watching her trying to recover from the shock of it, having so inadvertently exposed her friend. Hadn't the writers of those letters been real people to her before that, cranks and kooks rather, about whom I was being over-fastidious?

At that moment, I made my own decision. Though I don't intend to dispose of my papers for some time, having uses for them myself, when the time comes, those letters will be among my archives. For only when people can read the power and diversity of response to persecution will they begin to learn that the people in pain are, in fact, their good friends. The solution is not to throw their testimony into the fire, but to face it.

To read those letters is not only to recognize suffering but to encounter remarkable courage. No hate mail I've ever received has been signed. Apparently self-righteousness needs anonymity. But from those who had real reason to protect themselves, the letters have invariably been signed. They have been a support for me without which it would sometimes have been nearly impossible to go on writing. Preserving pain and courage and love betrays nothing but the world's hypocrisy. Our only real defense has always been the truth.

The Sex War

THE ATROCITIES MEN have committed against women are increasingly being used as evidence against not only the patriarchy and heterosexuality but against men as a category of persons. Whether it is Chinese footbinding, African mutilation of the clitoris, centuries of witch-burning, or contemporary wife-beating and rape, the message is that men have a deep fear and hatred of women which disqualifies them as loving and political partners in any effort to make the world a saner and kinder place.

Such arguments are not aimed at a male audience but at women who persist in "fraternizing" with the enemy, to persuade women that even our fathers, brothers, husbands, and sons are mortally dangerous to us. No matter how gentle and intelligent men may appear, the vast industry of pornography delights their fantasies and confirms their real desire, which is to brutalize us with everything from their dirty socks to their giant cocks. They are never to be trusted.

It is a view which has much in common with the opinions of institutions like the church and psychiatry, except that the opposite sex which is now being feared and hated is men rather than women. There is more historical cause, surely, and it doesn't do anyone any harm to be aware of crimes in the past and present, but to blame and want to ostracize or eliminate a whole category of persons because some of them are rapists and murderers is surely the real bedfellowing with evil.

To co-opt the bigotry from which we have suffered is as corrupting of our real power as to be co-opted by and become tokens of the patriarchy. We see in both extremes that a woman, in order to achieve recognition, has to be not better than a man but worse.

I do experience daily a great deal of male arrogance I could live without, and the best men I know are still part of the problem rather than part of the solution. But since I, who have everything to gain from a feminist revolution, find it very difficult to change a great many of my own attitudes and patterns of behavior, it doesn't surprise me that even men committed to feminism have a hard time learning how to live in those terms.

What gets in my way often is fear. To have that fear transformed into paranoia is no help to me at all. It is one thing to be reminded of real danger, quite another to be terrorized by the myth that all men are monsters. Once I had to invigilate an exam in one of those windowless lecture halls in which the lectern is at the bottom of a pit, tiers of desks rising away forever to a vanishing back wall. I was supposed to have two assistants, but neither had turned up. As I tried to get the exams set out, students began to shove at the doors and finally did break through: a hundred and fifty young engineers, flooding down toward me. The one who reached me first smiled and said, "It's late. Would it be against the regulations for me to help you?" Those barbarian hordes, intent on rape and pillage, suddenly looked like nervous students afraid of failing, far more my victims than I was theirs. We broke the regulations together.

Teaching a writing course, I had a number of male students turning in stories about rape, nearly all of them self-righteous and self-aggrandizing for the protagonist. One was a particularly clever satire about a young man trying to learn how to deal with the system by reading all the proper books and taking their advice. Confronted with the Kafkaesque nightmare of applying for a job in a large corporation, he gradually stops conforming and starts fighting back. At one point he has a wrestling match with a form he's supposed to be filling out; and though it nearly overwhelms him, he finally stabs it successfully in its marital status. His last act of triumph is to rape the secretary.

"Do you know what this story is saying?" I asked him. "This fellow isn't a hero; he's a victim, victimizing the person even less free than he is."

"But you're not supposed to think of her as human," he protested. "She's just another symbol of the establishment."

"I don't think women readers would see it that way."

What we have to fear and fight against is not each other but the garbage in our heads that can make us see each other as symbols of the establishment, as enemies rather than as people who must learn to break the regulations together.

I think there may be less hostility between gay men and lesbians than between straight men and women simply because not many of us try to live together and therefore face at close and daily range an imposed inequality that women no longer accept and men haven't yet learned to live without. Contrary to the cliché that we can be defined as man-haters and woman-haters, we may be an important source of genuine, if limited, intersexual sympathy, to bring this centuries-old sex war to points of peaceful negotiation.

Fucking Pariahs on the Schoolroom Shelf

MY IRONIC CONSOLATION, while friends like Margaret Laurence and Alice Munro battle with the would-be book banners over inclusion of their work in school curricula, has been that nobody has ever suggested my books be read in schools in the first place. There is a negative smugness in being a pariah. For this reason alone I was disappointed when I was asked just a few months ago to contribute a particular story to an anthology designed for the high school trade.

The story itself, of course, is blameless, not a shred of sex of any sort in it. It is, in fact, the only story about violence I've ever written. A woman looks out her window and sees in her garden a wounded man who is shortly shot by the police in the street below her house. She has to turn on the radio to find out that he is a bank robber who has shot a policeman. Her husband, reading the paper on the way home, is alarmed for her safety. They watch the events telescoped on the six o'clock news, then scenes of war, all of which seem much realer to the woman than what took place before her eyes in her own garden. It is called "A Television Drama."

Well, what did I expect them to choose? A story about happy lesbians? the unmarried young? a middle-aged woman who can't go mad? The only safe subject, among my many, is violence. I contemplate the potted biography: "Jane Rule is the author of a number of books . . . " The editor pauses, looking for a suitable title or two. Certainly not *Lesbian Images* or *The Young in One Another's Arms*. *Desert of the Heart* may be too suggestive. Even *Against the Season* has a rebellious tone. How about *This Is Not for You*? It's the one that's out of print and almost impossible to get.

I wasn't much of a reader myself when I was in high school. Though I had difficulty reading, at least part of my problem was the material we were assigned. In much of it I was being lied to, offended, and bored. Do schools still choose expurgated *Caesar* to "pacify" the boys, expurgated *Romeo and Juliet* as a cautionary tale for the girls? When I was a teacher myself, I was amused to discover that those who censored Shakespeare often didn't get and therefore left in the bawdiest of the puns while removing all references to pregnancy. People could commit suicide, gouge each other's eyes out, betray and murder, but copulate they must not. Watered-down Shakespeare was, of course, the best we got. Much of the rest was chosen not for its insight or beauty but for its uplifting and patriotic sentiment. I majored in English at university before I discovered writers who were important to me because I had decided to learn from the skillful liars the techniques for telling the truth.

There are, of course, students who don't have difficulty learning to read, who are encouraged not only at home but by particular teachers to discover writers who speak to their growing need to understand themselves and the world around them. But the majority are dependent on school texts and school libraries. Apparently only about ten percent of the population goes on borrowing, buying, and reading books. A ninety-percent failure rate to interest people in what can be found in books should indicate that there is something basically wrong.

Though the censorship of our own forum, the *Body Politic*, is a dramatic issue we must all actively involve ourselves in, the job is far larger. We must be vocal in our communities, on our school boards, in our schools, to see that not only Margaret Laurence and Alice Munro are available to students, but that even I am there, not only with my own small contribution about violence but with the hundreds of pages I've written about human relationship. The time for negative smugness is past, for accepting a censorship of ourselves, while schools are increasingly being pressured by people who think it wholesome to teach hatred, fear, and violence. Margaret, Alice, and I, along with dozens of others, belong on school library shelves and in school texts, teaching people that *fuck* (which still can't be looked up in most dictionaries) is not an act of violence but a word for another four-letter word, *love*, the most complex, engaging, and important subject in the world.

Closet-Burning

Coming out, all the way out, is offered more and more as the political solution to our oppression. The argument goes that, if people could see just how many of us there are, some in very important places, the negative stereotype would vanish overnight. Such a fantasy must occur to people young enough not to remember the rounding up not only of Jews but of homosexuals in Germany during World War II, inexperienced enough not to have witnessed the punishment of minorities simply because, like blacks and Indians, they are visible. It is far more realistic to suppose that, if the tenth of the population that is gay became visible tomorrow, the panic of the majority of people would inspire repressive legislation of a sort that would shock even the pessimists among us.

Since it is highly unlikely that such a day will suddenly come, there is not much point in feeling fearful; but even as an ideal, mass coming out is dangerous. As a moral club to threaten people still in the closet, it is far too effective, for most people who aren't in a position to defend their own rights feel wretched about it already. It is neither true nor kind to suggest that their silence is necessarily part of our oppression. The ideal must be, instead, a climate so changed that there really is no danger even for the most vulnerable. While those of us who can afford to and those of us who have been forced or have chosen to make sacrifices work to effect those changes in attitude and law, we should not join in a witch-hunt to expose others but protect and reassure those not equipped for the task.

The first and most important step any gay person takes is accepting that sexual identity as something not only natural but potentially joyful. There have always been some who have been gay and proud; but for every Natalie Barney, there have been many more Radclyffe Halls, accepting the degrading descriptions of psychologists, inevitable suffering, and a need for pity. The gay liberation movement, taking pages from the black and women's movements, has already made an enormous difference to a generation of urban gay people, but still to be reached are vast numbers of people who had to come to terms with their sexuality alone or in secret, who still suffer guilt or shame. For many of them, the support they need for self-acceptance can't come from the gay community alone but must include the understanding of parents, husbands, wives, children, coworkers. Until we have convinced the majority of people that the problem really is homophobia, we can't substantially help those in most need of it.

Contrary to some activists' scornful accusations, no closet, however richly furnished, is a comfortable place to live. Coming out for many people would mean what it has for John Damien: the loss of a job he loved, material comfort, and security; distress for his family. What he has now, along with a very precarious life, is a court case which has already gone on for years and may last many more unless it is finally dismissed and not heard because of financial pressures even John's most loyal supporters can't withstand. That John has been willing to make such sacrifices for his rights and ours requires hard gratitude from us all. We would be an ungrateful community indeed not to give him all the moral and financial support we can. We would be a blindly cruel community to ask such sacrifice and dedication of everyone in similar circumstances.

What we can ask of those who can't openly join us is help that is possible for them to offer: out of fear, out of self-protection, never betray others as a way of establishing your own innocence, either by frankly exposing them or by telling or laughing at homophobic jokes. Support, anonymously if necessary, all cases for homosexual rights before the courts, whether the issue is child custody or freedom of the press. Tithe, not in guilt but in hope, a tenth of your salary to the people who, by temperament and position, are able to work in the open for a time when it will also be possible for you. Finally, don't be apprehensive for those of us vulnerable to the backlash you anticipate as inevitable. We have burned our closets behind us, it's true. But the only thing we destroyed was shame. Some of us may face bankruptcy or jail, but no power on earth can destroy our proud self-respect which we keep also in trust for you.

Reflections

AT THE TIME a new novel is about to come out, I am always more aware of those inevitably disappointed people who want literature to be not only a mirror but a flattering mirror of themselves and their way of life. More often than not they see in my fiction a series of bad jokes on that old theme, "Mirror, mirror on the wall, who's the fairest of them all?" out of which my own voice comes, "Not you, pale face." In fact, there are probably too many handsome characters in my novels to be politically correct; but I am more apt to feel sorry about the trouble beauty causes people than to celebrate it, and I try to spare no one real life.

I do understand the appetite in the gay community for art which can celebrate, but too often that desire gets translated into a need for narrowly correct propaganda for one lifestyle or another. Any writer who tries to please such an audience is doomed to failure, because within the gay community there are not only different but morally and politically conflicting tastes. Celibates, monogamous couples, cruisers, sadomasochists, lovers of children, separatists, bisexuals, men and women cannot all be pleased at once. And sexuality itself is only one of dozens of tags by which we identify ourselves. Our religion or lack of it, our politics, our family backgrounds, our jobs, our landscapes, our handicaps and avocations are all important to us. Create a bad-tempered social worker and alienate a whole profession of readers. Suggest that art can be motivated by revenge and offend all romantics. Make a rich man moral and start a Marxist parade. And so on and on.

A good writer is not in the business of propaganda because the nature of art is not to generalize but to reach the universal by way of the particular. And there is a crucial difference. Anyone who sees *Macbeth* and comes away with the notion that all women are murderously ambitious for their husbands is distorting the intention of the play. What should happen instead is so clear a perception of the character of Lady Macbeth that her name becomes synonymous with that kind of female ruthlessness wherever it is met.

The difficulty for gay people as for other minorities is that we have so long been either ignored or portrayed in negative stereotypes that it is hard not to be a defensive audience even for our own artists, directing them to leave deformity, loneliness, vanity, insanity, and suicide to the homophobics who already relish any negative image available. Give us instead the fairest of us all, the gifted, the wise, the kind and the beautiful. People, whether they should or not, do generalize from literature; and we need heroes and heroines.

The heterosexual community got just that in the popular literature of the 40s and 50s, but those shining stars and Hollywood endings frightened and depressed more adolescents than inspired them, and fed a deadly cynicism in those who were already living happily ever after. No matter how wholesome the lie, it is part of the sickness, not of the cure.

I will not apologize for us, nor will I dress us up as the silverware ads of the 80s. I will not even give us my exclusive attention. I will bring to us, as I do to each of my characters, all the tenderness, severity, and humor I can command to show us making our various contracts with the world. My mirror is never a bad joke. In it, if you will look with compassion, amusement, and hope, you will find that your image is fair.

Grandmothers

I SUPPOSE EVEN a six-year-old could write about being "an aging lesbian," might even feel the need if she'd already suffered a couple of years at the hands of a heterosexual nurse, been reprimanded by a mother for picking forget-me-nots for the lady next door, and been told in kindergarten to stop drawing the same picture over and over again: a stick figure at the top of a pointed mountain. At forty-six I may find it harder, because by now the catalogue of mortal blows and pleasures is far too long and complex for a short entertainment.

I think it's probably a "masculine trait" to practice dying from a very young age. Anyway, it's always the boy children I invent who shoot themselves with their own bow ties, grab their arrow-pierced stomachs and fall to the ground; and most of the real hypochondriacs I've known have been men who at the first twinge of headache are convinced of spinal meningitis; at the gentlest fart; terminal cancer. I also have a hunch that fatherhood is a way men practice dying. Women don't seem as often to need to invent melodramatic premonitions of death, the house of the body so much a way station for other life that even those of us who do not give birth acknowledge the wasted blood, the monthly murder of some new soul for the sake of our own lives. Our bodies seem to practice dying for us without aid of our imaginations. It is only when women have imposed on them men's fear of dying that they are caught up in the vanity of pretending not to age, comtemplate suicide at my age for a lost womb, a second chin, bifocals.

I loved all my grandparents, but I loved the *bodies* of my grandmothers, both of whom suffered from arthritis as I do now. They were fragile and deliberate in the way they moved, and from the time I was tall and sturdy enough to be some aid, they used my body as brace or hoist. They taught me early how to touch pain and to comfort, because they were at the candid mercy of my love. From them, far more than from my marvelously ample-bodied and competent mother, I learned the close intimacy of flesh. When, as an adolescent, I was physically shy with my mother, I always had sweet excuse to touch my grandmothers, to brush their hair, to help them dress, to choose among their rings which would still traverse the swollen joints of what were to me their beautiful hands, accurate still with needle and thread, with cards, with flowers, accurate with requests. I found their faces lovelier than any others of my childhood because they were *made*, could be understood as the bland faces of other children could not, as even those of my parents could not, since they did not yet know themselves and masked their ignorance as best they could. My mother has that wondrous face now.

When I was twenty-three, I fell permanently in love with a woman who was not much younger than I am now, whose face had already begun to be defined by time, and who has stayed there fifteen years ahead of me for twenty-three years, half my life. At sixty she is more distinguished, more readable, more beautiful than she was when I first met her. The gap between our ages finally begins to close with the premature aging of my disease. In fact, it is I who teach her how to touch pain and to comfort. She sometimes has a moment of surprised envy at a child's heedless running across a field. I do not like some of the irritating limitations of an ailing spine. Not to be able to lift a child is a deprivation, but young Kate down the road will soon be tall and sturdy enough to offer me a steadying shoulder. The natural imbalance of our erotic energies, which has plagued, amused, and taught us patience with each other, is not as pronounced as it used to be. As the erotic fuses with the simply physical, we return together to a place which shares with childhood long moments in the present, no future hope of accomplishment as commanding as the sight of eagles in the high air or a sudden colony of mushrooms in the daffodil bed.

To become an old woman has always been my ambition, and it may be that my life span is to be short enough to make a speeding up of the process necessary. I have had a long apprenticeship as lover; and in the way I can, I will still carry out those patterns of courtship, but I am coming into a time when I must be the beloved of children and the young, who will measure their confidence in terms of my growing needs. As my grandmothers taught me the real lessons of erotic love with their beautifully requiring flesh and speaking faces, so I would wish to teach the children I love that they are capable of tenderness and of strength, capable of knowledge because of what they can see in my face, clear in pain and wonder, intent on practicing life as long as it lasts.

Publications of
THE NAIAD PRESS, INC.
P.O. Box 10543 • Tallahassee, Florida 32302
Mail orders welcome. Please include 15% postage.

Contract with the World by Jane Rule. A novel. 340 pp.
ISBN 0 930044 28 2 $7.95

Yantras of Womanlove by Tee A. Corinne. Photographs. 64 pp.
ISBN 0-930044-30-4 $6.95

Mrs. Porter's Letter by Vicki P. McConnell. A mystery novel.
224 pp. ISBN 0-930044-29-0 $6.95

To the Cleveland Station by Carol Anne Douglas. A novel.
192 pp. ISBN 0-930044-27-4 $6.95

The Nesting Place by Sarah Aldridge. A novel. 224 pp.
ISBN 0-930044-26-6 $6.95

This Is Not for You by Jane Rule. A novel. 284 pp.
ISBN 0-930044-25-8 $7.95

Faultline by Sheila Ortiz Taylor. A novel. 140 pp.
ISBN 0-930044-24-X $6.95

The Lesbian in Literature by Barbara Grier. 3rd ed.
Foreword by Maida Tilchen. A comprehensive bibliog.
240 pp. ISBN 0-930044-23-1   ind. $7.95
                                  inst. $10.00

Anna's Country by Elizabeth Lang. A novel. 208 pp.
ISBN 0-930044-19-3 $6.95

Lesbian Writer: Collected Work of Claudia Scott
edited by Frances Hanckel and Susan Windle. Poetry. 128 pp.
ISBN 0-930044-22-3 $4.50

Prism by Valerie Taylor. A novel. 158 pp.
ISBN 0-930044-18-5 $6.95

Black Lesbians: An Annotated Bibliography compiled by
JR Roberts. Foreword by Barbara Smith. 112 pp.
ISBN 0-930044-21-5   ind. $5.95
                                  inst. $8.00

The Marquise and the Novice by Victoria Ramstetter.
A novel. 108 pp. ISBN 0-930044-16-9 $4.95

Labiaflowers by Tee A. Corinne. 40 pp. $3.95

Outlander by Jane Rule. Short stories, essays.
207 pp. ISBN 0-930044-17-7 $6.95

(continued on next page)

Sapphistry: The Book of Lesbian Sexuality by
Pat Califia. 195 pp. ISBN 0-930044-14-2 $6.95

Lesbian-Feminism in Turn-of-the-Century Germany.
An anthology. Translated and edited by Lillian Faderman
and Brigitte Eriksson. 120 pp. ISBN 0-930044-13-4 $5.95

The Black and White of It by Ann Allen Shockley.
Short stories. 112 pp. ISBN 0-930044-15-0 $5.95

At the Sweet Hour of Hand-in-Hand by Renée Vivien.
Translated by Sandia Belgrade. Poetry. xix, 81 pp.
ISBN 0-930044-11-8 $5.50

All True Lovers by Sarah Aldridge. A novel. 292 pp.
ISBN 0-930044-10-X $6.95

The Muse of the Violets by Renée Vivien. Poetry. 84 pp.
ISBN 0-930044-07-X $4.00

A Woman Appeared to Me by Renée Vivien. Translated
by Jeannette H. Foster. A novel. xxxi, 65 pp.
ISBN 0-930044-06-1 $5.00

Lesbiana by Barbara Grier. Book reviews from
The Ladder. iv, 309 pp. ISBN 0-930044-05-3 $5.00

Cytherea's Breath by Sarah Aldridge. A novel. 240 pp.
ISBN 0-930044-02-9 $6.95

Tottie by Sarah Aldridge. A novel. 181 pp.
ISBN 0-930044-01-0 $5.95

The Latecomer by Sarah Aldridge. A novel. 107 pp.
ISBN 0-930044-00-2 $5.00

A VOLUTE BOOK
NAIAD PRESS, INC.
P.O. Box 10543
Tallahassee, Florida 32302

All Naiad Press Books listed in this book can be purchased by mail, as well as Valerie Taylor's three titles.

Journey to Fulfillment, A World without Men and Return to Lesbos
$3.95 each plus 15% postage and handling—minimum 75¢.

NAME _____

ADDRESS _____

CITY _____ STATE _____ ZIP _____

BOOK(S) _____

_____

TOTAL ENCLOSED $ _____